Dancing Nude in the Moonlight

Joanne C. Hillhouse

MACMILLAN CARIBBEAN WRITERS

MACMILLAN
CARIBBEAN

Macmillan Education
Between Towns Road, Oxford, OX4 3PP
A division of Macmillan Publishers Limited
Companies and representatives throughout the world

www.macmillan-caribbean.com

ISBN 1 4050 1269 2

Text © Joanne C. Hillhouse 2004
Design and illustration © Macmillan Publishers Limited 2004

First published 2004

All rights reserved; no part of this publication may be
reproduced, stored in a retrieval system, transmitted in any
form or by any means, electronic, mechanical, photocopying,
recording, or otherwise, without the prior written permission
of the publishers.

Typeset by EXPO Holdings, Malaysia
Cover design by Gary Fielder at AC Design
Cover illustration by H Ann Dodson

Printed and bound in Malaysia

2008   2007   2006   2005   2004
10   9   8   7   6   5   4   3   2   1

Series Preface

Dancing Nude in the Moonlight is a story of love between two cultures. It explores the hardships and tensions of immigrant life in Antigua, where newcomers from the Dominican Republic are met with suspicion and hostility. And yet, though the languages and ambitions of natives and newcomers differ, the two communities share much in the way of Caribbean culture and religion. Slowly love is nurtured between a single mother, the eldest of three young Spanish-speaking sisters struggling in poverty, and an aimless, has-been Antiguan cricketer who turns out to have an unexpected talent for sports commentary.

The Macmillan Caribbean Writers Series (MCW) is an exciting new collection of fine Caribbean writing which treats the broad range of the Caribbean experience. As well as novels and short stories the series includes poetry anthologies and collections of plays particularly suitable for Arts and Drama Festivals. There are also works of non-fiction such as an eye-witness account of life under the volatile Soufriere volcano, and another of the removal of an entire village to make way for an American base in World War II.

The series introduces unknown work by newly discovered writers, and in addition showcases new writing and favourite classics by established authors such as Michael Anthony, Jan Carew, Ian McDonald, G C H Thomas and Anthony Winkler. Writers on the list come from around the region, including Guyana, Trinidad, Tobago, Barbados, St Vincent, Bequia, Grenada, St Lucia, Dominica, Montserrat, Antigua, the Bahamas, Jamaica and Belize.

MCW was launched in 2003 at the Caribbean's premier literary event, the Calabash Festival in Jamaica. Macmillan Caribbean is also proud to be associated with the work of the Cropper Foundation in Trinidad, developing the talents of the region's most promising emerging writers, many of whom are contributors to MCW.

Judy Stone
Series Editor
Macmillan Caribbean Writers

The Macmillan Caribbean Writers Series

edited by Judy Stone

Novels:

Jeremiah, Devil of the Woods: *Martina Altmann*

Butler, Till the Final Bell: *Michael Anthony*

Such as I have: *Garfield Ellis*

The Boy from Willow Bend: *Joanne C Hillhouse*

Dancing Nude in the Moonlight: *Joanne C Hillhouse*

Ginger Lily: *Margaret Knight*

Exclusion Zone: *Graeme Knott*

The Humming-Bird Tree: *Ian McDonald*

There's No Place Like …: *Tessa McWatt*

Ruler in Hiroona: *G C H Thomas*

Plays:

Champions of the Gayelle: *(ed Judy Stone)*
> *Plays by Alwin Bully, Zeno Constance & Pat Cumper*

More Champions of the Gayelle: *(ed Judy Stone)*
> *Plays by Winston Saunders, Dennis Scott & Godfrey Sealy*

Stories:

Going Home, and other tales from Guyana: *Deryck M Bernard*

The Sisters, and Manco's stories: *Jan Carew*

The Annihilation of Fish and other stories: *Anthony Winkler*

Almost there ...

The sweetest part is
the anticipation
the knowing
being on the brink of
reaching for your joy
I hear the music
Otis belting *try a little
tenderness*
and I try to caress you
with my mind
reach for me
I need you.

– jhohadli

Thanks to God, family and friends for bringing me through, Macmillan and especially Judy for taking a chance on another book.

Special thanks to Gisele and Jane for your help with this manuscript.

1

Michael.

So it was true what Keats said, he mused in a kind of daze, bizarrely flashing back to the lines from one of his Uncle Wellie's many books. *"Beauty is truth, truth beauty – that is all ye know on earth, and all ye need to know."*

It must be true, because he looked into her eyes and saw the truth of his future unfolding before him. True passion. True commitment. Truly living. And everything else dimmed in its presence. The truth was hers was a spectacular face; dark eyes, skin the colour of a dark even tan, a snub nose, rose petal lips. If he had to describe it, an impossible task, he would say she most resembled those so-called "exotic" Mexican girls in those old Westerns they showed late at night on television.

But there was something angelic about that face, and a bit of the devil there too. A man could spend lifetimes peeling away the layers of that face and still never quite know its beauty. He wanted to drink that face and eat it, lick it, kiss it, consume it. He wanted to run his fingers through her silky-looking brown hair; to feel beauty's texture and tickle his fingers across love, touch love.

Michael had never felt that lightning bolt before, that *ping*, that *wuddup bap* that knocked you off your feet and knocked you back down again as you struggled to get up. He hadn't quite believed in it actually, but as he knelt, so to speak, dazed in its presence, how could he doubt it? Love at first sight, and second and third, ever after.

Love.

It seemed inadequate to capture all he felt at that first meeting. She had his heart, and they had yet to say one word to each other.

Pamela spoke up for both of them. "Selena, this is my PE coach at school, Mr Lindo. Everybody call him Michael but that's not his real name. He used to play cricket for the West Indies," she sang. The fourteen-year-old had a way of stringing *non sequiturs* together like most others her age that Michael had come across.

And as a coach in the secondary schools, following the injury that had ended his brief call-up to the regional cricket team, he had come across many.

The sister, Selena, continued to look at him, unimpressed. Michael began to feel a little like he had as a child when his mother would dress him in his best shirt and pants and a too-big tie from God-alone-knew-where that hung down to his hips, and take him "visiting" on Sundays.

"Visiting" meant calling on Tanty Lindo and other members of his father's family remaining in Antigua; people who didn't want anything to do with this *cruffy foot Dominican gyal from Ottos* who said her boy was part of their family.

His father had been gone by that time, to Canada. But his mother insisted that he know his family and get what was coming to him. And though Daniel Lindo Sr. had said the boy wasn't his, they couldn't deny the truth of his lineage when they looked at that heart-shaped Lindo face, slightly puffy Lindo cheeks, the Lindo chin dimple, the deep-brown penetrative Lindo eyes set against his dark dark skin. Though his colouring was from his mother's side of the family, there was no denying that he was one of theirs. But they didn't have to like it. He felt now as out of place as he had then, sitting on a chair in Tanty Lindo's living room – "not on my good couch," she'd remind him every week – in Coolidge. This was about as uptown as you could get back in those days, outside of Crosbies, Hodges Bay and Marble Hill that is.

He was that little boy again, begging for approval, and not quite getting it.

He could just imagine what his best friends Meetoo and Asha, who was also a cousin on his father's side and a black sheep in her own right, would say to that. "You always after the butter-skin and them," Meetoo would tease, half-serious, "all ar-you Antigua man just the same." Asha would tell him to stop "pay dear fu people company" because nobody was better than you unless you let them be. He would tell her to tell that to her mother who forever treated her like the stepchild to her younger brother, who was the biggest screw-up Michael knew. His buddy Deeno would make some kind of crude joke. Uncle Wellie would get to the serious questioning, staring him down for the truth.

But he was jumping ahead of himself, because Selena was the one staring him down now. And the way her face was set, he felt just like little Junior – the boy he'd been a lifetime ago.

"What you want?" Selena said, her English slightly more accented than her sister's.

He snapped back to himself. He wasn't here to stare at her all day like some fool, after all.

"You see, we're putting together this national female school cricket team. We're into training several afternoons a week. Down the road we hope to be playing exhibition matches across the region," he explained, trying for a professional tone. "I think Pamela shows some talent. A lot of talent actually, and I'd like her to play with us. So we needed to get your approval as her guardian. There'd be a form for you to sign. But Pamela thought I'd be better off speaking to you. Explaining things. Getting your approval up front."

As the time stretched on and he stood on the porch while she barred the entryway to the house with her slight body, he felt more than ever like Junior Lindo, a Jehovah's Witness or some other unwanted visitor all rolled up into one.

She didn't have the body he'd come to expect on women from the Dominican Republic: the hips flaring seductively, the rounded buttocks, the more than a handful breasts. She was built instead like a tennis player: the Anna Kournikova model, all soft curves. Her sister Pamela had an athlete's body, too, come to think of it, but more the Serena Williams model: shapely as well, but much more muscular. In fact, there was very little to recommend them as sisters. Pamela was darker than her sister but with hair that was partly blonde, like it had been bleached by the sun. And, seemingly, naturally so. It wasn't as soft as Selena's actually; more the texture he'd seen on black people of mixed ancestry; what they ambitiously called "good hair" because it was closer to white than the kinks in, say, his own head.

Selena looked to Pamela for some kind of explanation and they spoke briefly in Spanish. He'd learned that Pamela preferred to speak in English, the language of her adopted country, Antigua, while, at home, her sisters tended to embrace their mother tongue.

There was another sister, Celia. She was a tougher sell, Pamela said. But they needed only one signature, and Selena was the

oldest; plus, Pamela had whispered conspiratorially, "She's easy."
Though looking at the uncompromising stance of the big sister
now, he wasn't convinced.

Pamela had laid out the dynamics of their family in the
twenty-minute walk from Ottos School to their Kentish Road
home, which, as it turned out, wasn't more than ten minutes
from his mother's house in Golden Grove – though worlds
apart.

She'd also told him how Celia had come over from Santo
Domingo three years before with first Pamela and later Selena
following. Selena, the oldest, had been in Antigua only about
eight months now. Unlike the other sister, who worked at a hotel
as a maid, she had had difficulty getting a job. She was good
with numbers, Pamela said, and had hoped to get a cashier's or
bookkeeper's job and study accounting once her English had
improved. But the only opportunities had been as a cleaner or
waitress, and she didn't yet feel desperate enough to lower her
expectations. Besides, the baby kept her busy. She'd had the baby
shortly after coming over with her boyfriend at the time, Victor.
They'd parted badly since coming to Antigua.

These complexities of Selena's situation were not immediately
obvious, looking at her in her pink housedress and matching
fluffy bed slippers.

"She have to help with the baby," Selena said.

"I know, but it wouldn't be every day and it would be a good
opportunity for her," he argued in a rush.

Selena looked to Pamela, who rolled her eyes and sucked her
teeth, at which Selena's eyes flashed. Pamela translated.

"She have to work," Selena responded. "I don't work. I have a
baby. We need money." She said all this staccato.

He felt like he was being put on; like she was trying to pretend
she didn't understand so she could stretch out the pauses, size him
up.

"Work?" he asked Pamela.

"We make doilies and crocheted dolls to sell," Pamela
explained. "It doesn't bring in much money and I could do that
any time. That's just an excuse."

He couldn't quite form a mental picture of athletic, tomboyish
Pamela with crochet needle and thread in hand.

Selena's eyes flashed again at Pamela's last words, and she spoke quickly in Spanish. He didn't have to *hablar español* to grasp that she was chastising her unrepentant sister for saying too much or being too defiant. "Selena," he intervened.

She stopped talking and looked at him. "Your sister is good with a ball," he said. "I know because I once was. Cricket has mostly been a man's game though women are some of its biggest fans. And with a regional cricket team for women now in place, it's more incumbent on us to train our girls to meet the opportunities opening up for them. Putting in place the kind of structure that we have for the men is a first step; opportunities at the national level, you know, to help groom and shape the available talent. This is a window of opportunity for young girls. Now I can only ask, but I think you should give her a chance; who knows where it could lead? You understand about grasping opportunity."

She didn't answer, only looked at him in an intense, searching way, but he knew she had understood.

"Where's the paper?" she said.

Pamela fished it out of her binder.

Selena didn't even look at it, simply held it in her hand. "I'll think about it," she said, then disappeared inside.

2

Selena.

He came back the following night, after she'd signed the consent form and given it to Pamela to deliver to school. He came to thank her, he said. And just when she was at the point of wondering why he cared so much about this girl who didn't even know what cricket was before coming to Antigua, he asked her if she'd like to go to a movie or something sometime.

So that was it, she thought to herself.

That explained the strange look in his eyes the day before and his odd way of staring at her for long pregnant periods in a way that made her face hot and put her on her guard.

Well, he'd come knocking at the wrong door, at the wrong time, as far as she was concerned.

She was off men. Except for her baby, Silvano, that is. He was the only man worth anything: her joy. His father, Victor, out of her life a full two months now, could rot in hell for all she cared. She spat for emphasis over the back porch, where she walked rocking the baby in the noonday sun as she thought of these presumptuous men. They always felt she was to have. She knew she was beautiful. She had no arrogance about it, no interest in it really. It never kept men from hurting you; a father from disappearing without a trace; a first boyfriend from practically raping you; your lover/husband-to-be from cheating on you, lying to you or hitting you so hard it left you for weeks with a ringing in one ear. Beauty didn't protect you from any of that. It didn't make you strong or appreciated; only something to take, crush and suck dry like sugar cane or a chicken bone.

She wore no make-up, did nothing special with her hair and didn't much care for body-flattering tight clothes like the jeans Celia wore when she wasn't working. Selena wanted to count for something, not to be counted as somebody's prize. So, as far as she was concerned, piss on men and their obsession with her beauty.

"What's going on?" Pamela's voice behind nearly made her jump out of her skin. Solid as she was, the girl moved like a mouse: quiet and quick. Maybe that Michael was right about her suitability for sports after all, Selena mused to herself.

She'd completely forgotten that Pamela would be home for lunch soon. At least there was soup left over from the night before; she would heat that up. Pamela took the baby as they went into the kitchen. "What were you thinking so deeply about?" Pamela asked in English.

She knew speaking English was a burden to Selena; or her older sister acted like it was. But she persisted, submerging her own tongue to her desire to assimilate. By assimilating, Selena knew, Pamela hoped to escape the criticisms and stereotyping Antiguans put on her people. Stereotypes that they all looked and dressed like whores; all wanted their men (as if … !) and were good for nothing more than wild sex; and all were fit only to clean up after Antiguans and to pick up their garbage.

She didn't understand these people; they even begrudged the jobs Antiguans didn't want. She thought about going home often. But *Mami* had a new husband, a new family, a new life really, making it weird for the three daughters whose father had disappeared leaving her to struggle all those years.

The old family displaced by the new. That wasn't really how it was, she supposed, but that's how it felt sometimes.

There was always their *tia,* but she was much older than their mother and poor, and it was relatives like her they had come to help.

Celia, the middle sister, had been the first to come, making good money at the hotels and singing the praises of the opportunity and conveniences of the island, if not the warmth of the people.

She encouraged their mother to send Pamela. This was something Selena had thought their mother would never consider, but she had, citing educational opportunities, chances to learn English. These reasons, to Selena, didn't justify sending off your then eleven-year-old daughter to a country where you had never been. Learn English? They already knew English.

Maybe it was true that her mother's gruff new husband of seven years and the two sons that had come during that time were the focus of her new life, and their comfortable two-bedroom house was just too crowded for so many children.

Selena came because of Victor. He had had dreams of more dollars in Antigua. Everyone said jobs were easy to come by and paid well. They were to be married. She was having his baby. She followed him.

From her mother's house to his, to this home she now shared with her sisters. At twenty-three, starting all over again.

"My thoughts are my own," she told her little sister in Spanish.

"Did you check the classifieds today for jobs?" her sister asked in English.

"Don't you worry about that," she replied in *español*.

"You know, the more you use English, the more used to it you'll become," Pamela said.

Selena didn't answer, just started spooning out the soup. But Pamela persisted. "It makes it easier to get work," she said. "Particularly cashier work. They're not going to hire you if they figure you can't talk with the customers. Or do you want to be a security guard or housemaid, or garbage collector? Or worse yet, a hundred dollars a week sales clerk on Market Street? Those are the only jobs for Santo Dominicans who won't assimilate."

Selena placed a bowl in front of her outspoken little sister, took her baby and said, "*Comes tu sopa.*"

Then she left the room.

3

Michael.

Michael spotted Uncle Wellie from halfway across the field. The bowlegged strut on the only father figure he'd ever known was distinctive.

The presence in his life of his mother's brother had made the absence of his own father easier to take.

Uncle Wellie was a joiner by trade like his own father before him.

Uncle Wellie was a quiet, almost reclusive sort. Didn't bother people if they didn't bother him; content to spend his personal hours listening to old-school calypso, jazz or the blues – the only music he thought worth giving the time of day – working on his wooden sculptures (yes, he was a closet artist), running on the beach, or engaging in a game of catch or two-man cricket with his nephew.

"Hey, boy," he greeted Michael.

"Who you calling boy, old man?" Michael said grinning.

"Ooh, let me show you old," the old man said, picking up the challenge. And the game was on.

Apart from these afternoons together at the T. N. Kirnon School grounds, or a Sunday afternoon listening to Ella, Billie, Nina, Sarah, Dinah, Satchmo, Duke, Monk or, lately, Cassandra, at Uncle Wellie's, Michael's favourite thing to do with his surrogate father was take in a Test Cricket match at the Antigua Recreation Grounds.

They both had an appreciation for the game that went beyond watching great athletes in action.

Cricket, Uncle Wellie had told a younger Michael, was part of what defined them as West Indian. If African slavery was the chain linking them to each other and to "Mother" England, forever defining their relationship as subordinates to her, then cricket was what shifted the weight of those clanking chains. For on the cricket field, Uncle Wellie said, no one applied the lash like the

West Indies, in a style all their own. In simple terms, it was beating England at her own game, reclaiming some of what had been taken, in the most gentlemanly of ways.

"Always real friendly about it," Uncle Wellie said. "None of that rough-housing you see in other sports, but ain't no mistaking the blood in our eye or the steel in our backbone."

And standing head and shoulders above all others in this game of one-upmanship was Viv Richards, Antigua's own who, Uncle Wellie said, called to mind other black revolutionaries like Prince Klaas, Cudjoe, Paul Bogle, Toussaint L'Ouverture, Marcus Garvey and Malcolm X. He counted Malcolm, he said, because his roots – at least on his mother's side – were in the Caribbean, and that was good enough for Uncle Wellie.

Uncle Wellie had read about all these men. Perhaps the only thing he had more of than music was books. Name the topic and it was probably covered in one of the hundreds of books mounted high against his walls. He had every book ever written on Viv, and Michael had read them all.

Viv was his idol after Uncle Wellie; his mastery of the game, his grace under pressure, his ability to inspire those around him to greater feats, his classic performances that happened almost routinely, the sense about him as he stepped up to the crease that he was going to do battle for all black West Indian people. He and Uncle Wellie had inspired Michael's performance and attitude on the cricket pitch.

"So how's that 'girl thing' you got going working out?" Uncle Wellie asked as they sipped water after a sweat-breaking turn on the field.

"It's not that 'girl thing'," Michael said.

His uncle, he knew, was disappointed at how short his career with the West Indies team had been. But that couldn't be helped. And he loved working with the girls.

"I like it," he said.

"Well, that's the important thing," Uncle Wellie said. "You have to like what you do."

"You should know," Michael said looking at his Uncle out of the corner of his eyes. But Uncle Wellie didn't take the bait. It was an old argument between them; Michael insisting that his uncle ought to do more with his sculpture and his uncle blatantly ignoring him.

"So, how's it going?" Uncle Wellie asked again.

"Good," Michael responded. "I think I solved my bowling problem. Found this Santo Domingan fast bowler. Speed, power, control, she's got it."

"Well, that's good," Uncle Wellie said. "How's your mother? Still so miserable?"

Michael shrugged.

"When you goin' move out from there and get your own place? Is not like you hurting for money and is not like she starving for company. She got that godchild living with her, ent?" Wellie asked.

"Arlene? Yeah. I don't plan on goin' in no rent house though. I lookin' to get a piece of land," Michael said.

"At your age? What you be now? Thirty? You shouldn't be looking. You shoulda done have," Uncle Wellie said.

Michael didn't answer. Uncle Wellie knew how much his injury had set him back, as had his mother's fibroid operation. Not to mention how long he'd been at loose ends after being declared not fit to play and being booted from the West Indies side. Until the Ministry of Sports finally found a spot for him: schools cricket coach. That didn't pay much, and the team coaching paid even less; but he at least enjoyed his work.

Besides, he didn't like the idea of living on his own. He wanted a wife, children, the whole thing. He reminded Uncle Wellie of that. "So who stopping you?" Uncle Wellie asked. "Though who'd want some female takin' over their space and controlling things, I don't know. Besides, you don't need one of them in your house to be a daddy."

"You know how I feel about children outside of marriage," Michael said.

"Yeah, yeah, yeah," Uncle Wellie said, cheupsing. "So any wives in the picture, Mr Do-Right?"

And when Michael didn't answer right away he glanced at him quickly. "Oh, dear, " he said, shaking his head. "I knew your game was off."

"What! You've never been in love?"

"No."

"Bullshit."

Uncle Wellie shrugged.

"So who is she?" he asked after a while.

"The bowler I was telling you about? Her sister," Michael said.

"Aah, I knew there was a reason you singled her out," Uncle Wellie teased.

"No, she's really great. And I met her sister after I already knew I wanted her on my team," Michael rebutted.

"So, what make her the one?" Uncle Wellie said. "And don't tell me she's beautiful. Please, don't tell me your expectations are that low."

So Michael remained quiet because it was her beauty that had seduced him; and he knew little else beyond that.

Uncle Wellie looked at him for a long time, then sighed, "Well, that's as good a place to start as any, I guess. Don't want to spend eternity looking at no ugly woman. But if you're planning a future with this woman, I hope it's not only that that draw you."

And he left it at that, picking up his gear and beginning to walk away.

4

Selena.

"¿Quién es ese hombre tan feo?"

Wearing only a half-slip and a bra, Celia peeped through the light curtains at the front window.

"What man?" Selena asked back, still rocking the already sleeping baby as she got up to look, although she already knew who it was.

He'd been coming by often – nearly every day – since she'd turned him down. Usually, it was walking Pamela home after practice. But if there was no practice, he'd find some other excuse. He was in the area and just thought he'd drop in, which, while it was a common enough practice where she came from, didn't happen quite as often here.

Still, she smiled at his lies and brought him water or juice and allowed him to sit on the verandah and talk for a while. She didn't usually say much, but he didn't seem to notice. He seemed to like to hear himself talk. And she'd grown to like the sound of his voice. And, unlike her sister, she didn't think he was ugly.

She wasn't surprised Celia did, though. He was good and black. There was no escaping that. And that was the first thing likely to turn off her colour-conscious sister. But she found the richness of his skin tone beautiful. That and his lips. He had ripe lips – juicy-looking, but firm. She grew soft inside just watching those lips move. She could admit that. She had developed an attraction – that was, as yet, mostly physical – to him and those lips. That dimple in his chin, constantly winking at her like a little eye every time he smiled, didn't hurt either.

But another part of the attraction had to do with his persistence, and the fact that it lacked the pushiness and aggression of most men she'd known. He came by almost like clockwork despite her rejection, true; but he never again pushed her to go out with him. She liked that.

Tonight, as they sat – him talking, her listening as usual – he invited her to the next day's practice. That wasn't a date, really.

Her sister was on the team, after all. She said yes knowing that Celia was watching all the while from the window. Well, there was nothing happening and nothing to tell, was there? He was just Pamela's coach.

"*¿Quién es?*" Celia asked after he'd gone and they were in the kitchen setting up for dinner.

"Nobody," she replied. "Just Pamela's coach. He's been coming by now and again since Pamela joined the Junior Girls National Cricket thing."

"What for?" Celia wanted to know.

"I don't know," Selena replied, now becoming tired of her sister's questions. Sometimes it seemed Celia forgot who was the older sibling. "Why didn't you come out and ask him?"

"Hmph. He's after something," Celia shot back, "and it's more than just the time of day."

"Well, so what?" Selena wanted to know, "Who else is knocking down my door?"

"What about Silvano's *papá*? What about him?" Celia demanded.

Selena looked at her sister like she was crazy, thinking she must be crazy to think that she'd ever give a man who had hit her – a man they both knew had developed quite a reputation for his womanizing since coming to Antigua – so much as the time of day.

"At least he's one of us," Celia said. "I don't know about these Antiguan men. Apart from being black and ugly, they think we're all whores. They're just looking for what's between our legs. And they don't have nothing up front; and on top of that don't know how to use what little they have, I've heard."

"I haven't been with one of our own who did know how to use what they have either," Selena shot back. "There's nothing worse than a selfish lover or a selfish man, whatever the nationality."

"You don't know what you're talking about," Celia said, dismissively.

"Seems I ought to know my own experience," Selena said.

Pamela came into the kitchen then and they shut up and sat down to eat. Selena knew the conversation was far from over. She could feel herself being seduced, not unwillingly, by Michael Lindo and she knew Celia – who acted like she was the oldest – hadn't had her full say on that subject.

5

Michael.

When she started coming out to not only her sister's practices but his Parish League practices and games as well, the fellas teased him mercilessly.

"*¡Chica, chica! ¡Ven aca! ¡Ven aca!*" they mocked to his face. And even more ignorant shit was said behind his back, he was sure.

But he didn't mind them much. He'd always been able to render people's grinding powerless by either ignoring or laughing at it, helping them out if it came to that. Years before when they'd christened him Michael on the cricket field, just after he'd gotten his now defunct jheri curl, he knew it was meant to be tongue-in-cheek. But he'd chosen to take it as a compliment. After all, who had more moves and a better voice than Michael Jackson? Nobody, that's who. He took to wearing one of his mother's old yellowing white gloves and a denim jacket he'd outgrown, even in the hot sun. At school parties and the few house parties he'd started sneaking off to, he'd try out moves he'd been practicing in his room. Soon, the girls who liked his brown eyes and dimples anyway started calling him Michael. And the name stuck, not because he'd resisted it, but because he'd embraced it. He'd been tired of answering to Junior anyway. It wasn't even his name, nor was the name it filled in for. That belonged to a man he'd never met, who'd never wanted him to begin with.

He pretended now that he didn't know what the fellas were saying behind his back and only smiled at the stuff they dared to say in front of his face.

All their talk was just that: talk. Like the big talk on the block about how they did and didn't treat their women, and how many women they had. Half of them didn't have anybody of their own.

And if they did have a lady, for sure she didn't measure up to Selena's quiet yet powerful beauty.

And the more he came to know her, it wasn't just her features that grabbed him. It was everything he was learning about her.

The way, when she was quiet, reflective, her face seemed as gentle and beautiful as the ocean at rest with the potential to become just as tempestuous as that same ocean in a storm. The way a slight quizzical crinkling of her brow signalled she was annoyed at something. The way the popping of a vein in her neck hinted that she was holding something back and, when that volcano burst, make no mistake you would be scorched by it.

There was nothing solicitous about her; she wasn't bowing down before him or anybody for anything. Even if she was *begging lodging* in Antigua, she wasn't going to lick the soles of Antiguans for the privilege. Pride. That's what it was. It was there in the way she held her long, slender neck straight above her spine, and it was a beautiful thing to look at.

Still, at the same time, there was something so fragile and gentle about her; and the first time – on her porch, in the shadow of a hibiscus – she allowed him to kiss her some, something so warm and giving. When they broke for air – only because they needed it to live – the only thing he could think to say was, "Wow!" Like some schoolboy who was new to such things as kisses and soft embraces, which he wasn't.

He'd had plenty of girls in his high-school days and even more in his professional cricket days – less these past years because he wanted more and because most of the women he knew weren't much attracted to perceived failures or men on the downswing. Which, he knew, was how many saw him.

For all his skirt-chasing – and he'd done plenty – there'd been days when all he could think about was sex – he'd always made sure to protect himself. He didn't want any surprise babies like he'd been. So, at thirty, he was childless and still searching, albeit with a considerably quieter libido.

That first kiss on Selena's porch changed everything. He felt hotter than he'd ever felt in his life, like somebody had lit a fire in his body. He had to step back and let the cool night breeze hit his whole body, gaze up at the full moon for a beat or two before coming down to her face. She was smiling, kind of tentative, kind of happy.

"Oh, this is different," he breathed. Nothing on her face changed, so he wasn't sure she'd heard him. Or if she, too, even felt the intensity of the moment.

"I love you," he said, and it frightened him to say it. He'd never said it before. She simply nodded agreement. And there was no surprise or fear on her face.

6

Selena.

Selena was hard pressed to pinpoint when she'd lost control of this situation, or at the very least when she'd lost her mind. I love you, he'd said. I love you, her heart had answered, though she'd had enough sense to keep her mouth shut. She wasn't about to admit loving some Antiguan man she'd known barely two months. And she certainly didn't want to enter into another relationship where somebody else held all the power. She didn't even have a job yet. What she had was a baby and two sisters to take care of.

So why couldn't she stop thinking about him and that kiss, like it was her first?

They were sitting at Fort James: she, Michael and the baby. He had borrowed a friend's car and taken them for a drive. And she had to admit it was beautiful. They had stopped first at Paradise View and looked out over the island at all the lights. Then they had stopped to get some chicken and had pulled up on the beach at Fort James where they placed a sleeping Silvano in the back seat and ate.

But once the food was out of the way, then things got ... hmmm. Tense?

She was so aware of him sitting there next to her in the close quarters of the quiet car that she had to clasp her hands in her lap to keep from reaching across to touch him. She'd never felt such a strong urge before, not even with Victor. And she couldn't even say what it was about him that made her hunger so great. That kiss and those lips, sure. Hmmm, the way he spoke softly unlike the loud, obnoxious rumbling of most Antiguan men. She found they talked like the person listening was halfway to the other side of the island. It made her want to close in on herself to keep from being the focus of all that loud, demanding attention.

She liked that Michael spoke quietly. Not like he was shy, but like he was certain he had your full attention. Maybe it was that that made her want to lean into him, reach for him.

Or maybe it was the memory of him stripping off his dripping shirt at last Sunday's match to reveal the most beautiful body she'd ever seen on a man. Maybe it was that that made her so uncertain of her own impulses, so physically aware of him. Maybe it was that that made her want to reach to him and run from him all at the same time. There was danger of losing her heart here.

It had betrayed her before, and where it went her body wasn't far behind. Her last such misstep had landed her with a child whom she loved with all her heart, but who, nonetheless, had narrowed her world considerably, even as he broadened it.

True enough, this body and this vagabond heart had betrayed her before. She knew she was no innocent, and that once she fell for someone as she had for Victor, she wanted to give him everything in her power to give. That had always been her problem: holding anything of herself back for herself. That had changed with Victor, though. She'd just closed back in on herself like a morning-glory in the harsh light of the mid-morning sun. She'd always thought there was something sad about a flower so beautiful that bloomed for only a few hours before dying.

She saw too many similarities between it and the path of her own life so far; though she wasn't dead yet. The quickening of her pulse and the sweat on her upper lip were evidence of that. Here she was again in real danger of opening up, and at a loss to find the will to fight it.

"How's the job search going?" he asked, cutting in on her thoughts.

She shrugged. "My sister Celia says something will be opening up at her job soon. They're coming up on the busy season and they always take on more people then. By that time, they can't afford to be choosy. She said I stand a good chance of getting in then, with some day work at least."

"What kind of work?" he asked.

"Cleaning," she said.

"Thought you didn't want to do that."

She shrugged in response.

"Why leave your home to come here to do something you find so distasteful?"

Though his tone hadn't seemed vindictive, her temper flared nonetheless.

"Believe me, I'd go back home in a second. You think I like being here, having no friends, not being able to get a job and people I don't even know acting like they smell shit when I'm around? Believe me, the view from where I'm sitting isn't all that great."

His voice grew irritated. "Oh, come on, Selena, we're not as bad as all that. I'm your friend."

"Yes," she agreed, "but you want something."

And then, he went still. And she knew she'd misspoken.

She didn't know what to expect of his temper, so she waited.

He started the engine. She reached back for the baby, took him in her arms and hugged him to her like a lifeline. He squirmed uncomfortably, still asleep, and she eased up a bit.

When they stopped at her home, she reached for the door handle, but he spoke again.

"What I was building up to ... I know this guy," he began. "He's looking for someone. He's a photographer. He doesn't have much money to pay, about $300 a week. He'd be hard pressed to find anybody local to work for that. I could talk to him if you want."

"What would I have to do?" she asked without looking over at him.

"Man the studio. Deal with calls and bookings and such. Filing and distribution of photographs. Dealing with correspondence, mostly email inquiries. The hours aren't bad. Monday to Friday, nine to five, hour for lunch. And it's only about a fifteen-minute walk from your home. If you're interested, I can talk to him for you," he offered.

She wanted to hug him, but smiled a little smile, instead, and said, "I'm interested."

He nodded. "I'll let you know."

He reached across and opened the door for her but she didn't jump out right away. She reached down instead and touched, and lightly squeezed, his hand in apology, then whispered a thank you.

Celia was waiting for her just inside the door.

"Victor stopped by," she announced aggressively. "He wanted to know where you were with his son at this time of night."

"Celia, it's late," Selena sighed, heading straight for the room they shared with the baby.

"My point exactly," her sister hissed.

"Celia, this is none of your business," Selena insisted.

"You are my sister," Celia said, incredulous.

"And I am my own person," Selena said. "Who is Victor to call here checking up on me, anyway?"

"He is the father of your child," Celia said.

"And that's all he is, do you understand that?" Selena snapped.

"And this black ugly Antiguan boy, who is he? Tell me that. Who is he to you?" Celia wanted to know.

"Michael Lindo is a nice man and a friend. Black, yes, and also beautiful. And I like him, and that's all I am saying on the matter," Selena said, startling herself as much as her sister with that revelation.

"You're a fool, Selena. You always have been, walking around with your head in the clouds and rose-coloured glasses on. Too trusting. Too quick to open up yourself. I have more of a life than you and you'll notice I don't have any children yet. Have you never asked yourself why? Because I'm smart. You trust too much, too easy, give too much, too soon. Then you wonder why people take advantage," Celia was yelling now, causing Pamela to come running from her cot in the next room and the baby to start whimpering. "Celia, stop it," Pamela shouted, never one to let her sisters' seniority keep her from having her say.

"Go to bed," Celia snapped.

"No, you stop picking on her. Michael's a good man," Pamela said.

"Please! You're so desperate to be Antiguan, they could kick you and spit on you and you'd just bend over for more, still looking for the good in them," Celia snapped.

"You're so anxious to hate them all! Makes me wonder why you even bothered to come here, how you can stand to live among them, why you don't just leave," Pamela shouted.

"Really? And what would the two of you do? You still in school, her with a baby barely six months. I'm the only one bringing any real money in here. So think about that next time you're so anxious for me to leave," Celia shouted.

Selena sat on the bed crying and shushing the baby. She hated when they fought. And did Celia really think her to be such a weak idiot?

Later, when things settled down, unresolved, she lay on the bed next to her sister wondering how she had come to this point. Michael had come there for Pamela, had kept coming back for her. And somehow, she found herself shifting first from indifference to genuine enjoyment of his company to this ... this craving. Was it true, she wondered, was she just as weak and gullible as Celia said?

It was getting light through the window by the time her eyes started to get heavy, and by then Silvano was stirring and she got up to make breakfast for the family.

She wished she had *Mami* to speak to. Not *Mami* as she was most of her life – too sad over their father leaving to give much in the way of affection and too busy trying to make ends meet to notice what her children were lacking. But *Mami* as she'd been when she'd come up the week of Silvano's birth and taken care of her, of them all. She, Selena, had only just moved out from Victor's and in with her sisters.

She missed sitting over rice porridge with *Mami* in this same kitchen, sharing for the first time her fears about motherhood, and having *Mami,* who looked like Celia, only softer and older, telling her no matter how bad things got you just had to keep moving. When you stopped to let the weight of your worries hold you down, that's when you were lost, she said.

Selena's face had still been half swollen from the last time Victor had hit her, and she'd been scared. But her mother's presence, having her full attention for the first time in Selena's life, it seemed, had made her feel comforted for a little while.

She wished for that now but got only Celia trudging in, already dressed as the scent of frying eggplant lit up the kitchen. Her face was still set in the disapproving glare of the previous night. But Pamela – God bless her soul – came in already dressed for school, put her arms around both Selena and Silvano, and hugged them tight. Tears came to Selena's eyes. It would have to do.

7

Michael.

He woke to the familiar sound of gospel music playing very loudly, and just beneath that his mother's voice caught up, as always, in a mournful kind of praying. The first was actually kind of comforting. He'd woken up to those same *Radio Paradise* gospel standards all his life, and knew them all by heart.

The second made his heart heavy. Why did she have to be so sad all the time?

All his life, he'd heard his father's name repeatedly in those prayers and hated the man most in those moments. Hated him more than when he had to sit stiffly in Tanty Lindo's parlour wilting in the scorching aura of her disapproval. Hated him more than the many times he'd had to wear Uncle Wellie's old shoes to school in lieu of a new pair. Hated him because there was no joy in his mother's eyes. Hated him because somehow, over the years – and he couldn't say exactly when – he'd come to resent her because there was no joy in her eyes.

He and his mother rarely fussed. He left when her sorrow became so heavy it made him feel like he was trying to run through water, and when her ever-present voice lamenting the same story of betrayal became so loud it felt like it was right in his head. That's when he took off for Uncle Wellie's, or the nearest cricket field, or to Meetoo and Asha's apartment, or to a woman's house if there was anyone in particular at the time. Most often, it was Bethann, even if there was somebody else in the picture. At those times, he needed uncomplicated, and Bethann was that. He could lose himself for a while. They had known each other since school days, had both been plenty wild for a time, and had both, well, always found each other convenient.

But lately, his sanctuary had been Selena's front porch, sitting in the shadow of that hibiscus plant. There was sadness in her eyes, too, but behind that hope. And that gave him hope that if he could peel away enough of her protective layers, he could find his way to a soft centre where her heart nestled. That would be just like coming home again. Home like he hadn't felt since he'd been a baby in his mother's arms.

He hung in there because every time he saw her, and he didn't fully understand why, his heart leaped in anticipation of that promise. But Lord, she was trying. Sometimes he wondered what manner of fool he was, because as soon as he started to dare hope that his flower was opening up, she shut down, throwing up obstacles. Her lumping him together with all those men she said only wanted one thing had hurt. Maybe he had been that guy – maybe every guy had at one time – but he wasn't any more.

At first he'd been all set just to drop her home and forget about the whole thing. But sometime on the drive to her house, he'd cooled off enough to come to a different kind of resolution. He'd prove her wrong. He wouldn't pursue a physical relationship with her until he'd proven to her that he wanted more than that. Until they were both sure of his intentions. He could do patience. This one was labeled "Handle with Care", and he'd do just that.

"Hey, Uncle Wellie, you there?" he called. He knew he was. The loud music confirmed that. But Michael wasn't sure if he hadn't heard him bellowing outside the padlocked gate for the last five minutes or simply didn't want to be disturbed. Ella was on – in particular her playful, ad-libbed live version of "Mac the Knife". So at least he knew Uncle Wellie was in a good mood, which was why he kept calling. He could use some of that to pull him out of his worrying.

Finally, he jumped the wall fence and banged on the bedroom window. Then he heard Uncle Wellie swearing and stirring. Aah, he'd been napping. Well, so much for him being in a good mood, Michael thought.

"Boy," the man said irritably, eyes all scrunched up like it was the crack of dawn instead of well past midday.

"Hey, Old Man," Michael said, good-naturedly.

"What you want, Boy?" Uncle Wellie griped.

Michael just stared at him, his stance a little tentative, and he saw Uncle Wellie's eyes soften with a kind of resignation. "You need to find another sanctuary from your mother instead of intruding on people's Sundays," Uncle Wellie said, stepping aside to let Michael in.

Michael stepped around the grand sculptures that made the living room seem smaller than it was and headed straight for the fridge. He took one of the beers Uncle Wellie kept there although he didn't indulge himself.

"Too early for that," Uncle Wellie said, snatching the can and pouring them both home-made lemon juice.

"Health nut," Michael teased his vegetarian uncle, taking the drink. Nobody made local fruit juices like Uncle Wellie. Guava, hibiscus, sorrel. You name it, he could do it.

"So, what's for lunch, Old Man?" Michael wondered.

"Hm," was the only reply he got as Uncle Wellie began taking down pots from the cupboard and pulling his beans and grains together. Hard to believe they would all come together to make something edible, Michael thought, wrinkling his nose. But he knew they would.

He went back to the living room, took off Ella and dug up Uncle Wellie's *Otis Redding's Greatest Hits* album. He put on "Try a Little Tenderness", which, to his mind, was the best soul performance ever. It made him think of Selena, as he knew it would. He found an empty spot on the living room floor and closed his eyes to listen, barely registering his Uncle's grumbling about bare-faced young people who wanted to run other people's home and lives.

"Ooh, when she gets weary try a little tenderness," Otis crooned.

And Michael pondered how to do just that.

8

Selena.

Selena liked the new job. She was the only staff member, which suited her fine. Though far from overwhelming, it was challenging: the photo files were a mess and people were in and out or calling all the time about their pictures. Plus, her boss was a nice enough guy – a slightly flirtatious but soft-spoken Antiguan – who was hardly around enough to be much of a factor anyway.

The way he just dropped the running of the place into her lap and went on his merry way, it would've been easy to rob him blind if one were so inclined. For a family man, he didn't seem too bothered about money. If she didn't make it a point to go to the bank on Fridays, cheques would never get cashed or deposited. And she paid herself out of petty cash. It was bizarre.

After she'd been there about two weeks, Celia insisted on taking her out to celebrate. Her sister hadn't said much on the subject of Michael since their fight and they seemed to have reached an uneasy peace. But she didn't fool herself that Celia was at peace with that decision.

They went to Rosario's, accompanied by some of Celia's friends from work, including a Guyanese girl. Pamela was home with the baby.

"What are you drinking?" Celia asked over the loud music in the club.

"Coke," Selena responded.

Celia twisted her mouth into a sarcastic smile. And Mariluz, Celia's best friend in Antigua, joked while jabbing her in the shoulder, "Come on, Selena, you're not driving tonight. Have a *Presidente*."

But she'd never been much of a drinker, so she stuck with her Coke.

She was having a good time in spite of herself, and in spite of the fact that her sister's friends – who kept being lured onto the dance floor, drank plenty and laughed and talked loudly – were not really her crowd. She found herself relaxing into the spirit of the small downtown club where her home tongue swirled around her and the music was as familiar as the skin she wore. She kept refusing invitations to dance, nonetheless, until Celia, with determination, dragged her onto the floor.

As they danced with each other, it took her back to summer afternoons in her mother's living room in Santo Domingo when she and Celia – little girls then – would link arms and twirl each other this way and that in imitation of the expressive dances they'd observed the adults doing.

She'd always been moody, but she hadn't been as serious or timid then. That fear of jumping shoulder deep into her emotions had been a lesson of age and time. Back then she'd laughed easily, and Celia – though bossy even then – had laughed easily too, and they'd been just sisters and best friends, and that, too, had come easily.

And here at Rosario's, it felt good to pretend.

And then she saw him.

Victor.

He walked through the door looking as good as ever. His soft hair was longer and pulled back in a ponytail, a look that had been hot maybe five years earlier. But even this lack of cool didn't detract from his natural good looks – large light brown eyes, a nicely shaped nose, perfectly aligned cheekbones, and a strong chin. This last had been her weakness; she hated a man with a weak chin. Victor's problem was he knew he looked good, as anyone watching him stride in wearing those tight black jeans and unbuttoned print shirt could easily recognize.

He didn't spot her right away in the dark, as he moved to the bar with a short, heavy, red-skinned, red-haired girl in tow. Either his tastes had changed considerably or he wasn't very discriminating these days, Selena thought, a little bitchily.

She stopped watching him when she felt Celia's eyes boring into the side of her face. She pushed her way back to the table. The room had suddenly gotten uncomfortably stuffy and she wanted nothing more than to be home in bed with her baby pressed close.

Damn it, why did she even react that way to him? She knew if she had a choice she would never go back to him. Right? But her body still reacted to the reality of him, betraying her every time.

She was suddenly very mad at her sister, who must've known he would be here. What did she think would happen?

Selena sprang up suddenly. "I'm going to the bar," she announced. "Does anybody want anything?"

She saw Celia cock a shaved brow. *"Presidente,"* they all announced. And she elbowed her way across the dance floor and stopped directly across from him at the square-shaped wooden bar. His eyes widened in surprise and his lady friend's eyes followed his to rest on her as well. She smiled. But then the bartender distracted her by tapping on the bar. She ordered the four beers, counting herself in the mix.

Then he was at her side, his lady friend still staring at her from across the bar.

"When did you start drinking?" he asked as the bartender put the beers down and she pulled out her money.

"You don't know all there is to know about me," she said defiantly.

He smiled. "True," he said, his voice getting suggestive as he invaded her personal space. "But I know plenty." He licked his lips. She knew that little trick. And was pleased with herself for not responding to it; pleased that she, in fact, found it to be a bit of a turn-off. There was no naturalness to him. Everything he did came off like it had been practiced for hours in a mirror.

"Not any more," she said, scooping up the beers, two to a hand, and pushing her way back through the crowd.

On the drive home in the taxi, she found herself thinking about him; how once upon a time she had thought he was everything she wanted. He was beautiful – too fine-featured to be described as handsome exactly – and fun and a good lover: not because he was giving, but because he was a performer. But he was also spoiled.

The hitting hadn't even been the worst of it; it was the sense that she was losing herself, that that was the price of his love. She'd worried that some day she'd just disappear; just wake up one day and not even recognize the person she had become. Or even remember who she was, or what she'd wanted from her life.

"Walking down memory lane?" her sister whispered close to her ear. And she smiled at the irony that Celia's little ruse to make her face her memories had, in fact, succeeded, but with the effect of solidifying her resolve. Victor wasn't what she wanted, never mind her body's instinctive response.

9

Michael.

He was surprised she'd agreed without protest or evasions. There was a resolve about her lately, like she'd made up her mind about him. Still, he wasn't ready to test that resolve just yet by pushing for more than she was ready to give. So he took baby steps. Ice cream and an evening walk window-shopping along Redcliffe Quay. Going back to buy her a pair of earrings she'd admired. An outing to the Cathedral Cultural Centre when a dance company from Cuba came to town. A lunchtime picnic at the Botanical Gardens after stopping by *Zachariah's* for bun and cheese.

All very non-extravagant, all very non-threatening, all exceedingly pleasant.

She spoke about home more in these times: about her mother and two baby brothers – Juan Luis and Miguel – who were dying to see the baby. Her favourite thing, she told him, had been to sit out in the street after the electricity went off, which, in their area, was even more often than in Antigua, and share a drink with her mother (when her mother bothered to get off her feet for a minute or two, which was rare). They would watch and listen to the children play up and down the street, which saw hardly any vehicular traffic, listen to the music playing on some battery-operated radio at the shop across the street, hear her mother hum along. They didn't talk much, she said, even in those times, but still it was nice, companionable.

He had reciprocated by sharing his favourite thing: cricket with Uncle Wellie up at the T. N. Kirnon grounds. He told her how Uncle Wellie was like a father to him, the only father he'd ever known.

And they never asked questions, either of them; just accepted as much as the other person was willing to give. They had grown closer. He knew that to be true.

But still he was surprised when she agreed to an entire day.

He decided to take the route the big yellow school bus used to take on their annual school picnic years before.

They drove through Fig Tree Drive and he noticed how she looked around as though she'd never seen any of it before, which, come to think of it, she probably hadn't.

"Nice, isn't it?" he asked. This was his favourite bit of the country and he wanted her to like it too. "I find this part of the island to be Antigua as I know it and love it, remember it growing up. The people not in so much of a hurry like you find in town. They real friendly. Hell, even the landscape out here look innocent. All green. It's just nice." She smiled in what he took to be silent agreement.

They stopped at Wallings, where they had to climb uphill a bit to the old dam and the closest thing Antigua had to a rain forest. They walked a while in silence, then he promised that they'd come back here some time and go camping. He earned a look from her for that.

They then went back down the hill to his rented jeep, and jelly water from the vendor at the side of the road. And they drove on. He didn't want to take her to all the touristy places – Shirley's Heights and English Harbour and other old forts where white ghosts fought battles that had nothing to do with his people. So he detoured at Piccadilly and took the back way, along the coastline, to Bethesda and from there headed out to Half Moon Bay. That beach was always fairly deserted, being so far.

So it was, and so they swam. She told him how at home the beach was always so crowded with tourists that she didn't much like to go. "But this is nice," she said, with only a hint of nervousness at being alone with him.

And once the water hit her skin, it seemed to wash away all reservations. Her face took on this peaceful expression, like he imagined it would look after sex. It was a satisfied look. Blissful, even. He smiled, liking to see her happy. She didn't know how to swim, and the water was a little too rough for back-floating, but she waded and dipped herself and seemed content with that.

The urge to kiss her – despite his best intentions – was suddenly too much as he watched the water wash over, then pebble her skin, her face, her lips. He turned and headed back to the beach.

"You had enough already?" she queried.

"I'm just going to get a little sun," he said.

She tilted her head, taking in his dark skin. "I think you're done," she joked.

He smiled and continued up the beach. The sun was hot, but not too hot. He lay on his stomach, more to conceal his budding arousal than anything, resting his head on his arms. Soon, he felt a trickle of water down his back, and twisted around to squint up into the sun, and into her face – the face that had robbed him of words when he first met her. She seemed even more beautiful, because now she smiled and opened herself a little to him. She grinned now, teasingly. And he tried to read her. Was she telling him she was ready? Or did he risk sending her running again by moving too fast too soon? No, best to let her make the first move, and decisively so. So while he wanted to turn over, reach up and pull her down on top of him, he settled for smiling and turning his face back into his arms, leaving her to plop down on the towel beside him.

"What kind of sandwiches did you bring?" she asked. She had offered, but he had insisted on making lunch, wanting to show her that he could handle himself okay in the kitchen. Well, if tuna sandwiches and a garden salad, macaroni pie and baked chicken proved that.

They ate in silence, and by the end of the meal he was feeling a little sun drunk. He was starting to doze a little bit when he heard her say, "Thanks for today, Michael."

"Junior," he mumbled.

"Huh?" she asked, even as he wondered why he had just said that.

"Junior," he repeated, more awake now and studying her for reaction. "My name's not Michael, not legally. It's just a name I got on the block, decided to keep. I really carry the name of the man who fathered me. A man I never met. I prefer Michael."

Now, it was her turn to study him. Finally, she smiled, "Well, I like Michael. And I still say thank you, Michael. It's been a good day. I haven't had a lot of those since coming here."

"Well, it's not over yet," he promised, smiling sleepily.

They passed the rest of the day at the beach, going back into the water after resting for a while. He allowed himself the pleasure of holding her close and brushing her hair with his lips; but he didn't take it any further, not wanting to risk this fragile peace they'd achieved.

He hoped his final stop for the day wouldn't prove to be his undoing.

He'd told Uncle Wellie he'd stop by on his way home. They pulled up at the white wooden house, hearing the sound of old calypso music as they parked. He opened the door without knocking, knowing Uncle Wellie wouldn't hear him over all the noise. Besides, he was expecting him.

10

Selena.

His Uncle Wellie was just coming out of what seemed to be the kitchen when they stepped into the living room, which seemed to Selena, on first sight, to be more of an art gallery or a studio at least.

She found herself torn between staring at the beautiful wooden sculptures and greeting the squat, bowlegged man who had so shaped Michael's life. The sculptures all reminded her of black or Latino people dancing. They curved this way and that sensually, like he'd tried to capture a perfect musical note in each piece. They conjured up images of Carnival and really beautiful sex. Or maybe she just had sex on the brain. There was no denying it was all she'd been able to think about since Michael stripped at the beach.

"So you're Selena," Uncle Wellie said with a pleasant smile.

"Yes," she responded. "It's nice to meet you, Mr … ."

She didn't know what to call him. Michael had always referred to him simply as Uncle Wellie.

"Just call me Uncle Wellie, or Wellie if that too familiar for you. Everybody does," the older man said.

She smiled. "It's nice to meet you, Uncle Wellie. Michael has told me a lot about you."

"Oh, he can't stop talking 'bout you these past weeks. I was starting to think he made you up. But here you are. Just as pretty as he said. You could use some meat on them bones though. I never could understand the undernourished look that come to be so popular these days," Uncle Wellie said.

Michael shifted nervously, caught between wanting to laugh and not wanting to embarrass her, she suspected. She frowned a little, wondering if she'd ever get used to how these people just said whatever was on their mind.

He served up a delicious vegetarian soup in calabash bowls for dinner. And for the first time since coming to Antigua she really felt content in the company of Antiguans. She was sitting down to dinner with a family and they were talking about music.

It turned out Michael's Uncle Wellie had a number of Latin artistes in his sizeable jazz collection; people like Tito Puente, Chick Corea, Pancho Sanchez and Ray Barretto, as well as covers of Latin tunes by jazz greats such as Dizzy Gillespie. And before she knew it, she was swaying and tapping her feet to tunes like "*Oye Como Va*" in the middle of all those wooden statues; like them her body reaching for the next note.

As far as Latin music went, she was a greater fan of pop tunes and ballads in the vein of Marc Anthony or her namesake Selena. But at that moment, her body rocking and swaying, Chick Corea's "Spain" felt like the best music she had ever heard as the instruments dipped and dived, whistled and clapped all over the place.

"Your uncle is nice," she told him on the drive home.

"Yes," he agreed.

She opened her mouth but couldn't find the words to express what she felt, and it had nothing to do with the fact English wasn't her first language. When the car stopped outside of her house, she just sat there, still searching for the words. He watched her quizzically. And in answer she simply reached forward and drew him to her, kissing him. He hesitated only a moment before surrendering to the kiss, and she leaned in even more, the handbrake digging into her stomach barely registering.

He drew back, his eyes shining bright like a cat's, and in that moment she wished she had her own room, her own space, so that she could invite him in. More than anything in that moment, she wanted to make love with him. Instead, she sat and watched him get out and come around the car, open her door and extend a hand to help her out.

"I can't believe you neglect your child all day for some Antiguan man," Celia said as Selena slipped into bed next to her only minutes later.

Still smiling, she said, "Leave me alone, Celia. I didn't ask you to look after him, so don't worry about it."

Celia didn't answer, but Selena could feel the eyes burning into her back. However, she couldn't bring herself to care. She was too busy remembering the water on her skin, the kiss on her lips, the music working its way through her body.

"So how was your Sunday afternoon drive?" Pamela asked close to her ear as Selena made coffee the next morning. Celia had left earlier for work. She turned around to find her baby sister dressed for school and holding a freshly bathed Silvano.

She smiled, "It was nice."

"Just nice?" Pamela teased.

"Very nice," she amended. "I met Michael's uncle. He was wonderful. He has the largest music collection I've ever seen. We went all over. The beach was my favourite part of the whole thing. But Antigua has some really nice spots."

"And what about Mr Lindo?" Pamela teased.

"What about him?" Selena answered with mock seriousness. "Little girls have no place in big people's business."

Pamela only watched her, waiting. "He's nice too," Selena finally said with a teasing wink and smile of her own.

"That's all you're going to give me," Pamela demanded, "after I went to battle with Queen Bossy herself for you?"

"I'm afraid so," Selena said, her back still to Pamela, a smile still playing on her lips.

Michael.

The next Sunday was Tanty Lindo's birthday. "Why do I have to go again?" Michael asked his cousin Asha.

"Because I have to go," she retorted, as she sat in front of the vanity in the bedroom of her small Radio Range apartment.

"And why you have to go again?" he wanted to know.

She smiled at him in the mirror. "Because if I don't, I'll never hear the end of it from my mother. I mean, not that she goin' notice me much or anything with her perfect son Sunny there. But you can bet your ass I'll never hear the end of it if I don't show."

Asha was a legitimate Lindo. But like him, she didn't fit the mould of that proud Lindo lineage.

As Tanty Lindo was forever reminding them, her family came from good people. They were people with name and respectability. Her father had been an overseer on one of the bigger plantations in his day. "A black man!" she would say proudly, though the children had all seen her bleaching cream standing next to the milk of magnesia in the medicine cabinet.

Her own husband had been head teacher at the exclusive all-boys private secondary school, later chief advisor on education policy to the prime minister. Again, not an easy feat for a black man; although she always reminded people that he was at least half white and not a bastard either. No, his father had "taken" him, seeing to it that he got a good education and everything.

As she was also forever reminding them, her family was made up of people of influence, with friends of influence, no less than the now-deceased former prime minister himself. She and her husband had had audiences with Princess Margaret aboard the *Britannia*; not many people in or out of little Antigua could say that either.

That her husband was gone and she, though past retirement, had to be working still to make ends meet and keep the extensively mortgaged family house sitting in a community that, for all its former affluence, had seen better times, was never discussed; at least not in her presence.

Tanty Lindo intimidated Michael still, though he saw her rarely now that his mother wasn't dragging him up there to make them own up to the fact that he was one of theirs. But Asha had proven to be even more of an outcast than he was; well, almost. She had her grandfather's light colouring and had been thought very artistic and bright as a child. Now, as Tanty Lindo put it, she "ran around" with locks in her hair "like she don't belong to nobody," smoked, had dropped out of law school for a career as a multimedia artist, and didn't care about Princess Anne, the prime minister or any of her family's friends of influence.

Asha did her own thing; her teenage rebellion against a mother who treated her younger son like he was gold had evolved into a way of being. And her relationship with her mother was the one with which Asha still struggled.

So now, as they got ready for Tanty Lindo's birthday, Michael watched her fuss and fuss and fuss with her locked hair, head wraps and hair ties laid out around her. If he suggested to her that it did, in fact, matter a great deal what her mother thought of her, Asha would likely bite his head off and had done so more than once. She liked to think she didn't care what anybody thought. But she did.

"Why you didn't bring that Selena girl, create a diversion, take some of the focus off the two of us?" Asha teased.

"I wouldn't subject her to that. You mad?" he demanded. "I'm having enough trouble trying to figure out how to introduce her to my mother."

She stopped fussing with her hair and turned fully to him. "Your mother? This sound serious," she said.

He shrugged. "I think it might be, yeah."

"So how come I don't meet her yet?" she wanted to know.

"I trying to give it to her in small doses," he said. "I don't want to frighten her off. She met Uncle Wellie. They seemed to hit it off. He cooked. We listened to music. He even had some Spanish music."

She turned back to the mirror. "So tell me something, anyway. All them Antigua woman round the place; why is a foreign gyal, a Spanish one on top of that, you choose to go with?"

He looked hard at her. "What kind of talk that?"

She jumped quickly to her own defence. "I not saying nothing 'bout them; it just …"

"Antigua woman like seamstress; they cut too much style," Michael cut in.

"What about that Beatrice one? She come off like she was ready for anything you was ready for," Asha said.

"Bethann," he corrected.

She dismissed that with a wave of her hand. "Same difference."

"And I don't know what you bringing her up for anyway," Michael said. "Is not like you ever liked her. Or anybody else I ever dated for that matter."

"That's cause they're all dutty foot," Asha replied, unrepentant.

"Well, if is so, why you bringing up Bethann now?" Michael asked. "As if I could see myself married to a woman like Bethann who done give it away to all and sundry."

"Married? Who talking 'bout married?" Asha demanded, whirling around and narrowing her eyes. "And I won't even mention that you just proved my point 'bout the calibre of woman you accustomed to dating. I won't even call you on the little double standard you spouting 'bout woman sleeping round while you doing the same damn thing. What I want to know is how married enter the story already. Michael, I hope you not letting this girl push you into nothing, nuh."

He laughed at the irony of that. "Believe me, if anybody pushing, is me. Selena don't want a thing from me. And nobody nearly talking marriage yet. I just saying she's the type I could picture in my future, long term, you know. I felt that way almost since the minute I met her. I never felt that before."

"So what's the appeal?" Asha persisted. "Since she's not a dutty foot like Bethann, who you decided wasn't good enough. What? She's a virgin? I remember from experience how you all men like that particular challenge."

"You can remember that far back?" he teased, and she threw a bottle of hair oil at him.

He ducked, laughing, but she wasn't smiling. She looked deadly serious now, the teasing and scolding a distant memory. "What about her so?" she asked.

Michael got up, restless now. He never much liked all this talking about feelings that women seemed to go for. "I don't know,

Asha; I don't have words like that. I just know is her. You never been in love?"

She turned back to the mirror, shrugged her shoulder. And he smiled a little as he went to sit next to his cousin and friend. "Is just that, Ash," he said, "is love. There's no explaining it."

Tanty Lindo was in fine form, sitting in the big printed red armchair like a queen holding court. Michael had to admit she was a striking woman. One thing about Tanty Lindo: she had presence.

He remembered, as a small boy, listening to her tell stories about events here and there at which all the boys had lined up to dance with the best dancer and the best looking girl in the set. And she didn't give them the time of day either. They had to come good.

When he looked at her these days, though, he had a hard time picturing that girl. Her face was as he had always known it, unsmiling. Her mouth had that faint twist which implied she smelled something funny and that it just might be you.

Then all of a sudden, like a rainbow breaking through a cloudy sky, Michael saw her face light up as he had never seen it do before.

His face turned, as did those of others in the room, to the distinguished-looking older man who had just entered. "Maurice," Tanty Lindo gushed – that being the only word he could think of for it – rising as she did so from her throne. "Clarissa," the man boomed. Soon the two were embracing in the middle of the room while everyone stood around waiting for an explanation.

"So, that's Maurice," Asha mumbled next to him.

"Who's Maurice?" he asked.

"Tell you later," she whispered back.

Meanwhile, Maurice – whoever he was – and Clarissa – which Tanty Lindo apparently didn't mind this man calling her – had taken their show to the couch. She looked like a young girl – eyes bright, smile wide, cheeks swollen with happiness. She was beautiful.

Michael found himself wondering why she couldn't look like that all the time; and he became more and more curious about who this Maurice was.

They were talking only to each other, heads close, and everybody went back about their business pretending not to notice

Tanty Lindo caught up in this person whom she hadn't even bothered to introduce.

Michael did manage to pick up bits and pieces of the conversation, however, and his ears perked up when he heard, "I saw your boy, Danny, not more than two weeks ago. He's a fine-looking man. Looks just like you. How long has he been in Canada now?"

"Forever, it seems like," Tanty Lindo responded, her smile dimming slightly. "Close to thirty years. Only been back twice, and never brought his family even. Only time any of us get to see him is when we go there. And I don't like to travel any more."

"But now is when you should be travelling, now that the children are grown and the grandchildren too," Maurice said. "Your life is your own again."

"Please, I'm old now," Tanty Lindo protested.

"Old? What is old?" said Maurice, loud enough now so that everyone could hear. "You have as much life ahead of you as you want. If you're old, what should I say? You look as sweet to me as that girl in her white lace dress with the yellow sash, remember that, and the stars in her eyes."

And Tanty Lindo blushed, something Michael would have bet good money he'd have died without ever seeing.

"He's the one that got away," Asha said, somewhat derisively, on the drive home. She was in a pissy mood. Close contact with her mother tended to do that to her. For the life of him, Michael couldn't figure out why she let her mother – overbearing as she could be – affect her so.

"Got away?" he asked.

"I heard my mother talking about it once. I'm not sure how she know, because Tanty Lindo not one for talking 'bout these things, but maybe as the oldest she pick up things, you know," Asha responded.

"He used to go with her a time back. Before she choose Papa Lindo – or her mother chose him for her, anyway. In them days, it was all about marrying right, you know. And this Maurice wasn't nobody. But the feeling was that he had loved her and she had loved him. And he was bright, they say, but he didn't have no family or nothing. You know, he didn't have no name, not like Papa Lindo. He was a scholarship student. They say when he left for Canada, he asked her to go with him, but she wasn't having it.

Say she not leaving Antigua to get swallow up in Canada where nobody know her."

Michael shook his head in wonder. "One thing I can say, I never see her smile like she smile today."

"Yeah, well," was Asha's only response.

"He mention my father," Michael said.

"I heard."

There were pictures of his father and his Canadian family alongside the other family pictures in Tanty Lindo's living room.

Michael became quiet and Asha's eyes strayed from the road over to him. "I don't know why you waste time thinking 'bout him anyway."

He didn't answer. She pushed some more, "Ent is you say how your mother always cursing, saying how he took off right after she tell him she pregnant with you?"

He sank deeper into his own thoughts and didn't answer. He was more than familiar with Asha's view on the subject of his father. "Don't know why you want to waste time thinking 'bout a man who turn his back on you," she said again.

"But then you have your mother *and* your father," he shot at her.

"Michael, please," Asha argued back. "You notice Sunny wasn't there after all. Where you think he is? Back in rehab. In and out, in and out. That's my brother. You want to know what my mother spend the whole time talking to me 'bout? Why I don't learn how to hold on to a man. Sydney, who she didn't even like, because for all his opportunity, he not doing nothing with his life but hanging round his mother shop, dipping into the cash register and looking sharp. That's who she want me to hold on to. Everything I do, for that woman is an opportunity to criticize. Meanwhile, nothing Sunny do is wrong."

"Asha, please; spare me the whining, okay, you have a mother and a father," he said. "And everybody mother criticize! Is the law of nature, so get over it."

She shot him a sullen look and, worn out with the day and the conversation, they both sank into the distraction of their own thoughts, a tense silence enveloping them.

12

Selena.

The sisters were whispering heatedly back and forth in the kitchen.

"I can't believe you," Selena said for the tenth time.

Celia shot back, "What? He's my friend too. If I want to invite him over for breakfast and he want to spend some time with his son, what?"

Selena sighed heavily and counted to ten in her head. It made no sense arguing with Celia, anyway. She just did what she wanted. Victor was here, and he would eat breakfast right here in her dining-room, and there was nothing she could do about it at this point.

Cup of steaming sweet coffee in hand, she went back out to the dining-room; Celia would follow with breakfast.

She watched him, his hair pulled back as usual, playing with the baby, lifting him in the air, smiling and cooing at him. Silvano was delighted, smiling that dimpled smile that never failed to light up his face. Selena felt her aggravation ease a little. The man had a right to see his son, after all, and Silvano deserved nothing less than his father in his life. It was more than she had had most of her own life.

He put the baby down on the floor and came to sit at the table when he saw her come in with the coffee. "Thank you," he said, smiling pleasantly.

The smile that stretched her face felt more like a grimace, but he seemed satisfied with it. Celia set the food in front of him and they sat on opposite sides of the table watching him eat. Celia had that look of pride on her face – or was it fulfilment – that she had seen women like her mother get whenever someone – in particular, a man – was enjoying a meal she'd prepared.

"So, Victor, how are things going?" Celia asked. "You were working on that construction site out at Golden Sand Hotel, eh? I heard about the trouble out there."

"*Sí*," Victor said, talking with his mouth full. "The labour commissioner wanted to create a fuss about us working out there. Said the job should go to Antiguans."

"Please! Antiguans don't want to work," Celia scoffed.

"Celia," Selena chastised.

"It's true," Celia insisted. "I work with a lot of them. Every little task is too much. And they're always quick to call on their union."

"*Sí*," Victor said. "That's why my contractor … he's Jamaican … he say he prefer to work with foreigners, but mostly Dominicans. He don't like the hassle with the unions."

"But the labour commissioner shut you all down, eh?" Celia asked.

"Not for long," Victor said, lifting up the baby, who had crawled to his chair, and beginning to feed him bits of bread. "The heat will shift. There is always work. That's one thing I love about this country."

"The Antiguans don't seem to think there's always work," Selena said quietly.

"That's because they're too picky," Victor said. "Money is money. I work. Carry shit if I have to. Weekend come, I can wash it off and put on something nice and go dancing and forget about the shit I have to lift all week."

"Just as long as you remember to send some pampers and a little money for food before you go dancing. Babies need money, too," Selena interjected.

"Selena," Celia chided.

"What? It's true! For all his boasting about hard work, he seem to think raising a child is free," Selena said.

"Work comes and goes," Victor said, singing a different tune. "Money not always there."

"That is so true," Celia said. "It took Selena so long to get work."

"Where are you working now?" Victor asked.

"At a photo studio," Celia interjected.

"What, you taking pictures? You're a big shot now," Victor said, laughing at his own lame pun. "So, you don't need my money."

"I never needed nor wanted anything from you, Victor," Selena said, rising. "Your son, now, is another matter."

A strained silence descended on the room. "I have to change the baby," Selena said, lifting him from his father's lap and retreating to the bedroom.

She lay in there after changing the baby and listened to them laugh and talk in the front room. And without willing or wanting it, she found she was crying a silent tear or two. It was hard being around Victor and being thrust by her own sister at a man who had hurt her so deeply.

She fell asleep, tears drying on her face, Silvano resting against her side.

Something nudged her foot. She opened her eyes to her sister's disapproving face. "Why do you have to push so?" her sister demanded.

"I was about to ask you the same thing," Selena answered, easing up onto her elbows. "Why can't you just accept that Victor and I are not good for each other?"

"Because I can't accept that you think this Michael character is good for you!" Celia shot back.

"You don't even know him," Selena protested.

"I don't need to; they're all the same," Celia said. "They have no use for us."

"And is that any different than how we feel about them?"

"It's not the same," Celia said. "We became that way in self-defence. You remember when I first started at that hotel. Twice I was assaulted, and twice nothing was done. Remember when I had to sleep over because it was late and that night manager came into my room to see what he could get? He wouldn't take no for an answer, because everybody here thinks we're so easy. Because some of us work in the whore houses, we're all whores in their eyes."

"Michael has never treated me like a whore," Selena insisted. "He has been such a gentleman. Gentle and nice and very, very hands off. Trust me."

Hope shone in Celia's eyes. "So you haven't slept with him yet?" she asked.

"None of your business," Selena said quietly.

Celia sighed and lay down next to her sister. "I just want what's best for you," she said softly.

"What's best for me is what I want, not what you think I should want," Selena insisted, just as quietly. "That's not love. And Victor never loved me. And no amount of shoving him down my throat is going to change that."

Her sister was silent for a long time. "So you love this Michael?" she demanded. "Is that what you're saying?"

"I don't know if I love him," Selena admitted. "I know that I like him, and he's very good to me. While Victor is busy boasting about his job and having money to go dancing, and not paying any regular money to support his child, I know that Michael is the one who helped me get work so that I could stop feeling like I'm living off of my little sister."

"Selena, that doesn't matter," Celia said. "We're sisters."

"I know it doesn't matter," Selena replied. "But I didn't like it."

Celia sighed again, and Selena sent a pillow crashing into her face. "And stop sighing so much," she teased. "It's not the end of the world if everything and everybody doesn't fall into Celia's plan. Sometimes people just have their own minds."

"Hm, well, I just hope some people know what they're doing," Celia shot back.

13

Michael.

She looked beautiful in the moonlight. Radiant. All shadow and light and bright eyes. Where the shadows fell, they served only to enhance. Except for the shadows in her eyes that is.

"What you thinking 'bout so deep?" he asked her.

She looked at him then and smiled, and the shadows retreated. "*Nada,*" she said in her own tongue.

"It's beautiful here," she said in his.

They were at Ffryes. It wasn't really safe these days but he couldn't resist. He didn't have money for a hotel, and he wanted to be alone with her. Fort James, while more convenient, was too popular. Half Moon Bay, one of his favourites, was too far. He only had his friend Deeno's car for a few hours, and he didn't want to spend half of that driving. After a day in the company of his family, he really wanted to be with her where it was quiet and beautiful. And that was Ffryes bathed in moonlight with Selena blooming in its glow.

"You want to go in?" he asked her.

"Well, I didn't know we were going to the beach," she said. "I would have worn a swimsuit."

He stood. And reached down to pull her up. "We don't need swimsuits," he said, moving the dance forward while gauging her reaction carefully to see if she was keeping time. She seemed a bit nervous, and looked very young in that shy, tense moment. Then she leaned in and kissed him, and he forgot about the water, which was now lapping at their feet, and the moon, which had slipped behind a cloud, and the cool breeze and the beautiful setting. Part of him worried at his powerful reaction to her, but the greater part of him luxuriated in the experience.

The kiss deepened. And when they broke for air they were both breathing hard and flushed, even Michael with his deep black skin. And they kissed again. And the dance advanced with hands, tongues, whole bodies finding a common rhythm.

This time, when they broke, he went – her hand in his – to the car, where he retrieved a blanket. Working together they spread it where sand and vegetation met, using stones to keep it in place. Then they were kissing again, the blanket for a bed with only the moon as witness.

Michael took his time, too, kissing where each item of clothing had touched as each was removed in turn; teasing nipples with a playful tongue; dipping into her belly button and causing her to shiver before dipping even lower, and the shivers were joined by sighs.

The grazing of a sweet spot with the rough surface of his tongue caused those sighs to turn to moans and her back to arch as Michael tasted his fill of her. She was as sweet as he'd always imagined.

When he returned to her embrace, their limbs interlocked and danced as if to a mid-tempo calypso rhythm – slowing only for the necessity of putting on a condom. And Michael felt so alive, kissing cheeks, lids, lips as they moved.

And when the dance peaked, he felt like he was flying, jumping over the moon, as the cow did in that silly nursery rhyme.

And after, as they lay there, sweat cooling on their bodies – Selena with a Mona Lisa smile on her face – Michael searched her eyes for the shadows, and they were gone. "What are you thinking about?" he asked.

"That I feel good," was her immediate reply, and soon he was smiling that smile too, like he knew a secret the whole world didn't.

14

Selena.

Selena was nervous. She couldn't help it. These were Michael's friends. She wanted them to like her. And while she sensed no overt hostility, there was a kind of wariness. They doubted her, maybe, or her intentions, anyway, towards one from their circle.

They were at his cousin Asha's apartment. Asha and her friend and roommate Meetoo had cooked. Rice and red-bean peas, potato salad, coleslaw, and pork chops. The usual Antiguan Sunday fare, or so Michael told her. Although he confessed that his mother had been partial to shark on Sunday. The smell of it cooking had made him hate Sundays all through his childhood he had admitted.

She suspected, however, that he'd hated Sundays for lots of reasons, not the least of which were the post-Mass visits his mother insisted on making to his Tanty Lindo's.

She'd asked him if it was just shark he hated or all seafood. He'd shrugged, saying he could eat most seafood but didn't particularly yearn for it. He loved barbecue chicken, he said. And spinach rice. And pepperpot. And, on a rare, rare occasion fungi hot from the pot with a side of cassi and conchs. Oh, and he usually liked whatever his Uncle Wellie cooked. Mostly though he inhaled junk food; fried chicken and fries grabbed here, pizza grabbed there.

At that, she'd teased him about the example he was setting for the children he coached. He'd laughed and said he could still outlast any of them.

His cousin and her roommate were fair cooks, Selena decided. But she would have to cook for him sometime. She didn't like cooking and serving and all that as much as Celia and her mother, but she could handle herself okay. And she found the idea of perhaps doing it for him appealing.

"Selena, where you? You in dreamland?"

That was his friend Deeno, whom she found a bit too loud. Actually, when she surveyed the group, she couldn't much see how Michael fitted in. She supposed he knew Deeno from the playing field since he played in the Parish League with Michael. He had the same kind of loud abrasiveness, even in this quiet setting, that they all had on the field. Except Michael, who was all steely, quiet concentration at the pitch; nothing showy about him ever.

Meetoo was the anti-Deeno, an extremely quiet, red-skin, mousy-looking girl. She had intelligent eyes, though, and an unnerving way of staring at a person. She wasn't hostile exactly, but not welcoming either.

But Selena knew these weren't the ones to win over. Michael's best friend, apart from Uncle Wellie, was Asha. She remembered him telling her how they had bonded early over the fact that they both didn't fit into the Lindo world, even though she was legitimate. She was the kind of woman that made Selena nervous. She seemed so sure of herself, and was the only one who seemed up to the verbal sparring with Deeno. Selena suspected that their current argument, the one Deeno – whom she had to admit seemed a friendly sort – was trying to draw her into, was an old one between them.

"Some of you all women too nuff, Jack," he said, turning his attention back to Asha. "Me nah have enough thread fuh sew up all dem style all-you does cut."

Meetoo smiled at that.

"What, we just supposed to open sesame for every lame line you-all come with?" Asha asked. "We have to weigh the situation properly."

"We have to have this battle-of-the-sexes diatribe every time you two get together?" Michael wanted to know.

"You can talk," Deeno shot back. "There's a reason why you ain't hang on to none of them difficult Antigua women."

Neither Asha nor Michael seemed to take to that comment. Michael shot Selena a look, and Asha got up and started clearing with nothing more than the big chuups she felt the comment deserved.

Selena jumped up to help. "It's okay," Asha said, automatically.

But with a bright smile, Selena persisted. "No, please, let me help."

Asha shrugged. Together they made short work of the few plates and glasses without a word passing between them. It wasn't until

Asha was taking the after-dinner wine out of the fridge and setting the wine glasses that she addressed Selena.

"Don't mind Deeno," she said. "His mouth usually kick in before his brain engage."

Selena smiled at that, and Asha stopped and stared at her.

"You don't talk?" she asked. "I don't think I've heard your voice all day."

Selena shrugged, confessed quietly, "New people make me uncomfortable."

Asha started screwing the cork from the bottle, "Yeah. I guess I can understand that. That's the part I hate about a new relationship. Meeting the friends and family. It's one of those milestones, you know. All of a sudden, you not just dating any more. It's serious."

Then she gave a little teasing grin, which Selena wasn't entirely sure was an innocent one. "Don't worry; this is the easy part."

"The easy part?" Selena enquired.

"Well, Michael's mother," Asha said. "She not easy."

"What's your mother like?" Selena had to ask as they stood on her porch that night, saying their goodbyes after Deeno had dropped them off.

"Why you ask?" Michael countered, the question coming as it did out of left field.

Selena shrugged. "Asha mentioned her earlier."

Michael wiped his hand across his face and leaned back against the gallery rail. "What she said?" he asked.

She shrugged again. "Nothing really. She just said she's not easy."

"Well, that's true," he said, then sighed again. "Okay. Remember I told you how I never met my father? How he took off before I was born?"

Selena nodded.

"He didn't want me," Michael pressed on. "And I guess ... well, no, not guess, I know, she wasn't considered good enough for him by some of his people."

"Like your Tanty Lindo?" Selena asked.

He smiled. "Yes, just like her. If you ever meet Tanty Lindo, you'll see. A person's station, colouring, family background – all that is very important to her. Nowadays, she really kinda laughable, because them things don't much matter any more. But basically, she didn't want her son with this woman.

"As I tell you, my mother sort of force me on them. I still wasn't really taken in as one of them, but she made it near impossible for them to deny me.

"Not that the association ever brought me anything. Anything I ever got in life I got on my own. And I guess that's the thing I would tell my mother if I could ever get her to listen to anything I have to say: 'Stop dwelling on what people do you, or what life didn't give you and just get on with it.' She bitter, Selena. She's the most bitter woman I know, and she been that way long as I've known her."

Selena felt a strange kinship with his mother, this woman she'd never met.

"I can understand that. Sometimes …," and she paused and smiled. "Well, until recently, I thought we existed for men to husk out and throw away. I've seen it happen with my mother. When my father took off she was left with the three of us. Leaving was never an option for her. Then she got married again. And the man was good to her. He stayed around, you know. Gave her two boys. Provided for all of them. They had a home, better than a lot of other people.

"But I remember resenting him anyway, because it was like she got swallowed up by him. Things she never used to do, like smoke, she did because he did. Things she used to do, like go to church, she stopped, because he didn't. And it happened so subtly, you almost couldn't notice it.

"She's a good, capable woman, but her life became about the men in her life; first her new husband, then the boys.

"And then my experience with Victor. I know how love, if it's love, can eat you up. Somehow, it don't ever seem to eat up the men, you know. It can make a woman bitter."

A feeling of melancholy had settled over her, and he pulled her in close, still leaning against the railing. He kissed her lips lightly, put on a teasing smile. "I wish I could say I identify. But till now, I never been in love. And I have to tell you: it not nothing but sweet."

And she found herself smiling in return.

15

Michael.

Michael and Uncle Wellie were sitting on the front porch, newspapers spread around them, as they feasted on roasted peanuts fresh from Uncle Wellie's coal pot arch. Latumba, another defiant calypso voice, was Uncle Wellie's choice of music for the day.

> *"Answer me*
> *Answer me*
> *Do you like what you see?*
> *Did you vote for it to be …"*

"I think my programme going get cut," Michael said. "Matter of fact, with the axe coming down hard on everybody, I not even too certain 'bout my job."

Uncle Wellie didn't seem surprised by this. "I tell you 'bout working with government," he scoffed. "Bunch o' vagabonds. Now they done squander people money – they belly big big and they face fat fat – is the same poor people they want to pay. I tell you, injustice will never done."

"Come on, Uncle Wellie, times hard all over," Michael said, not much liking talk of politics.

"Come on, Michael, you spend too much time round me growin' up to still be so naïve," Uncle Wellie chided, his tone an echo of Michael's. "I mean, I know them Lindo people wouldn't say word one 'bout this government, though the foundation cracking round them and they principles. But I would've hoped I rub off on you a little bit."

"I just don't like all them political rhetoric, especially in the face of certain unavoidable economic realities that not only hitting us but everybody," Michael returned. "Next, you going to be going on about the 'damn foreigners' taking all the good jobs."

Uncle Wellie laughed at this last bit of sarcasm. "Love give you new perspective on things, boy?" he teased. Michael blushed.

"Look, I not about to fault nobody for seeking a better life," Uncle Wellie said when he'd sobered up. "Plenty of us elsewhere doing the same thing, with more likely to leave before this dry weather over. Hell, I did the same thing coming here. Can't blame nobody for trying to put food in their family mouth by good means or foul. Furthermore, they don't promise me nothing and they not the ones supposed to be looking out for me. Cussing foreigners, as far as I'm concerned, is firing your ire after the wrong set of people. Is them vagabonds that we elect who owe us an explanation. Is them I want reparations from, not some long-time slave owner I never meet."

Michael laughed at this. "Uncle Wellie, you're a case," he joked.

"In any case," Michael went on, "we not dead yet. In fact, we going to Dominica for a match next weekend. I just kinda see the writing on the wall, you know."

"Well, that already put you ahead of the game. Most people like they can't see past the end of them broad, flat nose. Now is just for you to prepare for it."

Michael sighed. "Is days like today I wish I was still with the side. Especially the way they performing these days. Even at less than a hundred per cent, I'm sure I could do a better job than them boys."

Uncle Wellie scoffed again, "Another bunch of vagabonds!"

16

Selena.

Next to her sister, Pamela was practically bouncing out of her seat with excitement. Selena had the window, but Pamela kept leaning over her to take in the lush greenery below. Selena was more concerned about the movements of the plane. They were on the last stretch into Dominica, the island below them as green and dazzling as an emerald. But all she could think was how much she hated flying and how she especially hated doing so in these little planes where you could feel every air pocket.

Her stomach was clenching, and she wasn't entirely sure that bent over her was the safest place for Pamela to be just then.

"What a beautiful country," her sister said enthusiastically. Selena glanced out of the window again, a distant part of her mind agreeing that, yes, the home country of Michael's mother was, indeed, beautiful; breathtaking, really. She was at the moment looking at the back of his head as he sat alongside another of the parent chaperones.

The nasal-sounding flight attendant announced that they would be landing momentarily, and reminded everyone to fasten their seat belts. And not a moment too soon, as the plane chose that moment to do a significant dip. A screech escaped Selena's lips but, thankfully, she wasn't alone, as some of the other girls had a moment of worry, too, before going back to their talking and laughing. Children, she thought drily to herself; a part of her envying them their flexibility, how fleeting worry was in their world. Pamela was like that. She didn't ever remember being as carefree as her little sister. Pamela was confident, not easily embarrassed, street smart without being wary of people. Secretly Selena wished she could be more like her little sister, who balanced all of that assertiveness with a healthy dose of sensitivity and compassion.

While sometimes she found herself wondering where Celia had sprung from, so great the chasm between them seemed at times, she knew Pamela was someone she would have liked to have as a friend even if they had not been sisters.

"Sit back," she told her little sister now. "Fasten your seat belt." Pamela got cheeky. "*Sí, Mami.*"

At that reference, she found herself wondering how Celia was doing. No one had been more shocked than she when Celia agreed to keep the baby for the weekend. It was a holiday weekend back in Antigua, and she knew how her sister loved to party. And the fact that Michael, who her sister still only tolerated in her life, was going to be along on this trip couldn't have sweetened the pot. But somehow she'd agreed without much fuss.

Selena sat back with a sigh as the plane landed. She was determined to enjoy this weekend. When Michael had told her he'd gotten one of the hotels to sponsor the tickets for the girls and their chaperones and that he would pick up her living expenses, she eagerly accepted, mildly surprised that she had reached the point in their relationship where she could accept a gift from him without feeling obligated. The thought of that made her smile. She really did like Michael a lot, apart from the fact that she seemed to have fallen in love with him.

"Bet I know what you smiling about?" her little sister teased, following the trajectory of her eyes to the back of Michael's head.

"Look, little girl," Selena said with mock seriousness.

Pamela laughed, as the plane settled on the ground, and Selena was feeling a hundred per cent better about the days ahead.

The ride to Roseau was long and treacherous, along winding country roads with the sea on one side and precipices on the other. But it was green and mountainous and a lot cooler than Antigua.

The guest house they were staying at was within walking distance of the school where the match was to be played; of everything really. So they found themselves that night at the Kentucky fast food place for dinner. The adults were wiped out, but the teenagers were still going strong. Somehow, though, they managed to herd them back to the guest house and into bed. Selena was sharing a room with the other parent.

She didn't see Michael again until breakfast and didn't get to talk to him until around midday, at the end of their morning practice session. And then, they didn't really talk, just sat on the grass watching the girls run around. Reflecting on the practice session, Selena thought how much she liked watching him on the field, whether it was coaching or playing. He seemed so much more alive then, so physical. It wasn't just the shorts he wore, or the sweats damp with his perspiration. It wasn't just that his skin glistened, that he was in constant motion. It was that he seemed happier than she ever saw him … except in moments of passion, of course.

"So that's the smile," he rumbled next to her.

"What?" she asked, startled out of her reverie.

"Pamela tell me you keep breaking off into a silly smile at the strangest times," he said. "I think I just glimpsed it." And she elbowed him lightly, slightly embarrassed. "Say what you want," he continued, "with that sister of yours around, I know somebody's in my corner."

17

Michael.

He'd never danced with her before, so this had turned out to be his favourite part of their trip. They'd won their match, the Dominica team not proving to be much of a challenge. And now, on their last evening here, they were in time to catch the last night of the World Creole Music Festival. So far this night, they'd seen acts from New Orleans, Canada, Africa, and were now enjoying the frenetic beats of Dominica's favourite sons – favourites in Antigua, as well – WCK. Selena was rocking against him, the first time all weekend they'd been with each other in a way that suggested she was more than just another parent on the trip. Everyone else was having too much fun to notice or comment.

They left shortly after midnight, though if the pattern held the concert wouldn't wrap up until the late morning hours. However, they were chaperoning teenage girls and had an early morning if they were going to get to Cane Field in time for their flight.

There was so much more he wished he'd done with Selena while they were here; bathed in one of the island's many rivers, gone hiking, rafting, visited the Carib reserve. It seemed like their weekend was ending too soon, and he hadn't had nearly enough time with her.

He found himself yearning to spend a full night with her in his arms, or vice versa. They'd never been able to do that. Neither of their living situations allowed for it. Even when they'd rented a hotel room, it had only been for a few hours.

He wanted more, and sensed that she wasn't far from that either.

Their first night together after getting back home, he broached the subject. "What you say we get a place together?" he said.

"We can't afford that," she said. It wasn't quite the answer he was looking for. "What you mean?"

"You were telling me just the other day how uncertain you were about your job with all the government cut-backs," she reminded him, "and I don't make enough to support us. We can't live on love, Michael. And what about Silvano? You really ready to live with an infant? Now that he's moving about confidently, he's into everything. It's not easy, believe me. The other day, I was at the sink and he managed to tip over a whole bowl of water onto himself. I was so frightened. All I kept thinking was suppose that water had been hot. Meanwhile, he's there wet and grinning. And though I was laughing I didn't know if it was from fright or because it was funny."

"You must really hate this idea," he said drily, feeling rejected. "That's the most I've ever heard you talk at once."

"Michael, come on ..." she began.

But he cut her off. "Forget it; it was just an idea. Look, I have to go. I have an early practice in the morning."

He got up from the bed and started pulling on his clothes. "Come, let me take you home."

She got up without further argument. The ride home was quiet, the goodnights abrupt. He felt wound up. He'd never considered even moving in with a woman before. It felt strange to be so certain about something, only to have it thrown back in his face.

After dropping off Deeno's car, he walked home, though his friend had offered him a ride.

On the long walk, he found himself cataloguing the failures of his life. A failed cricketing career; a has-been at thirty. A job and a programme he really cared about at risk. Still sleeping in the room he grew up in at his mother's house. This last one was particularly galling, especially since it brought him full circle to what was burning him. He'd asked the woman he loved to share his life and his home and she'd turned him down.

She hadn't said, "No, I won't move in with you," but she might as well have.

He turned up at his mother's house, and found he didn't want to go in. Even in the moonlight, he could make out how shabby and run-down the place had become. It could do with a coat of paint, but he hadn't been around much lately and simply hadn't taken notice. The front step was cracked and sinking. He needed to fix that.

He went inside. His mother was awake in her room and praying. He went to his room; lay down. The praying swelled and continued until it felt like it was right there in his head, in his blood, under his skin. He shifted restlessly in the bed. Sometime later, of its own accord, his hand leaped up and banged against the thin partition. "Mom, I trying to sleep," he declared loudly.

But, after a stunned pause, that only started another round of praying, with his name now being dragged into all that was wrong with her life. He got up with a disgusted, frustrated bellow, pulled back on his clothes and slammed out of the house that suddenly seemed too small and too heavy with sorrow to contain him.

He walked thirty minutes to Uncle Wellie's place, only to find the house in darkness, the gate locked, and hear Billie Holliday's "What a Little Moonlight can do" whispering out on the wind. More than likely Uncle Wellie had company and wouldn't take kindly to being disturbed.

He walked down to the beach, and there he sat, feeling the cool wind calm him.

"The girl right," Uncle Wellie said over breakfast the next day. Bread and cheese, and hot cocoa.

"What you mean?" Michael challenged, feeling slightly betrayed.

"Look, boy, what you have?" Uncle Wellie demanded. "You still live in your mammy house, and you thirty years old. I bet she still wash you clothes. The two of us know you don't cook for yourself. You don't have no place, no prospects that she can see, and you want her come struggle with you. She done been down that road from what you tell me. The thought of going there again bound to frighten her."

Michael was affronted. "I'm nothing like Victor."

"Boy, don't just hear my words, listen to what I'm saying," Uncle Wellie said, his voice getting softer, a signal to Michael that he was getting irritated. "It's too soon. You nah season yet, and you want she step in the pot with you. The food go taste too raw."

18

Selena.

Celia was chatting lightning speed about her cleaning service idea, but all Selena could think about was her fight with Michael. It wasn't that she didn't think about being with him like that, too. It wasn't that her living situation with her sisters was not less than ideal. She just knew the idea scared her, and she couldn't quite put her finger on why, her ramblings of the previous night notwithstanding.

"Selena, you're not listening," Celia accused, her voice breaking through her sister's consciousness.

"Sorry, what?" she said, sipping on her now lukewarm coffee.

"Look, I really think this is a good idea," Celia said earnestly. "I want to know what you think."

"I think starting a business is risky," Selena replied. Pamela entered the kitchen just then with a freshly bathed Silvano.

"Sometimes risk is good," she pitched in.

"Little girl, why you always in big people conversation?" Celia said.

"Hey, I'm on your side," she defended.

"Well, I wasn't talking to you," Celia said. "You running late for church anyway."

"I don't see why I have to go when you two don't," Pamela argued.

"Because we're grown-ups, and you are a child," Celia said. "Now, hurry up. And don't forget to take a bottle for Silvano."

"Yeah, yeah," Pamela said.

After she was gone, Silvano with her, Celia said, "She has a point though. Sometimes to get to your dream you have to take a little risk."

"And this is your dream? Cleaning people's homes?" Selena asked.

"Look, little Miss Better-than-Everyone-Else, I know you have some lofty ideas about yourself sometimes, but reality is a little messier than that," Celia snapped, irritated. "I want to get paid and if people want to pay me to do that I see nothing wrong with it. Probably why you can't hold on to a man, too."

That last remark stung more than usual in light of last night's fight, and she snapped back, "I can do without the kind of man you want me to hold on to, Celia."

Celia sighed, "Look, I'm sorry about that remark. I don't want to have that stupid fight again. I just want you to get off your high horse and see that this is a good idea."

"Well, if all you wanted was for me to agree with you ... sure, Celia, go ahead, Celia, great idea, Celia."

Her sarcasm brought a snarl from her sister, "You know what, Selena? Never mind. I'll go ahead taking crap from people and cleaning their shit. Does that suit your vision of how things should be?"

"How is this any different?" Selena asked, genuinely baffled.

"I'll be working for myself, not collecting a salary," Celia said. "That's how."

Selena sighed. "Okay, tell me this idea again," she requested, admitting that she hadn't really been paying attention when Celia spoke about it the first time.

"It's a service for working women," Celia said. "Mariluz and I were thinking ..."

Selena raised a sceptical brow at the mention of her sister's best friend, but kept her mouth shut at the look that earned her from Celia.

"We'd have a series of regular clients who we clean for weekly. We'd put together a network of freelance cleaners who we hooked up with these clients and we'd take a cut ..."

Selena shot Celia another look at this, but her sister rushed on. "And no, it's not pimping. We're more like agents. Plus we do most of the regular jobs ourselves. And that's not all; we also have a babysitting service. You know how much Antiguan women love to go out at nights. We have a network of sitters they can draw on. The beautiful part is, there's really no start-up capital involved. There's no office, no cleaning supplies to be bought ... that's all supplied by the client. We know enough women looking for regular work outside the system. And as for the clients, Victor said all we really need is a cell phone and some ads in the classifieds. Word of mouth will do the rest."

"Victor? He's mixed up in this?"

"Selena, don't start. Victor works a lot of homes, he has a lot of contacts. He can help us get jobs."

"Well, you certainly sound like you're sold on the idea."

Celia sat down heavily across from her sister, seemingly worn out by her previous frantic pacing. "I'm tired of working for the hotel, Selena. I have to put up with too much nonsense. I'm not getting anywhere. Yes, I do like the idea of taking charge of my own affairs."

"Even though it may be illegal."

"Illegal how? I have a work permit."

"What about a business licence?"

Celia was quiet.

"And you really trust Mariluz and Victor?"

Celia was quiet.

"Look ..." Selena began.

But she didn't know what to say and soon fell silent herself.

The sisters sat like that for a long time in their little kitchen. Finally, Selena got up with a sigh and went to the sink to begin washing her coffee cup.

"Just be careful, Celia," she said. "I understand why you want to do this. You think I don't, but I do. I just don't ... Just be careful. I don't know Mariluz very well, except what I do know doesn't exactly inspire my trust. It's not that she's bad exactly, but she's flighty, you know. Not grounded.

"And I know Victor can be charming and seductive, but, you know, so can a snake. I know what he did to me, and I know if it wasn't for Silvano, and growing up without a father myself, I wouldn't want him anywhere near me. But I know you. And I know that if there's a way to make this work, you can. Just don't let Victor con you into doing anything underhanded; just stay as above board as possible."

Celia got up and came over to her sister. "You know, the person I'd really trust to do this with is my smart-with-numbers big sister," Celia said with mock seriousness. And for a minute Selena seriously thought about it.

"Sorry, Celia, but this isn't exactly my dream," she said finally.

"Big surprise there," Celia said with a laugh. "Mami always said you thought you were better than everyone else. Didn't want to get your dress dirty. Always trying to get everyone to behave. Wouldn't eat from people; wouldn't even eat certain things Mami cooked. Wouldn't use the bathroom at Tia's house."

"What, that hole in the ground?" Selena snorted.

"That one, she think she's Queen Isabella!" Celia said nasally in an imitation of their mother's much older sister.

Selena smiled at this. Celia put an arm around her sister. "This may not be the lives we dreamt of, Selena, but we're not little girls any more."

"I know, I know," Selena agreed. "And I hope this works out for you. I really do."

Later that day found her in the beautiful garden behind the Antigua National Bank, where ninety per cent of the island's wedding parties ended up to capture the romance and beauty that they sought to immortalize the most important day of their life as a couple. She was operating the still camera, brought along because Cecil, her boss, was operating the video camera. She didn't really have a lot of experience on camera, just portraits in the studio.

But the client wanted both still and video memories, and Cecil was too cheap to spread the wealth. She'd learned some things during her time with Cecil about lighting and shot composition and so on, plus she had a genuine interest, which always accelerated learning in her case. But that he would trust her with a wedding! It made her almost nervous enough to put thoughts of her argument with Michael and her worry about Celia from her mind. Almost.

19

Michael.

Only Pamela and the baby were home when he got there, so he waited on the porch for her return. Pamela had invited him in, but he declined. He'd never been inside her home, and, suddenly, with things not right between them it didn't seem like the right time to push past that milestone.

Pamela had sat outside with him for a while, chatting away about nothing as teenage girls can. But then the baby's fussing for his dinner had sent her inside. It was just as well. He wanted to be alone. He was too nervous and worried for small talk.

A car pulled up in front of the house. It was Cecil letting Selena out. He waved at his friend. Selena walked up to the porch looking like a rose; a yellow rose in a pretty lacy top and an ankle-brushing skirt of the same material. She wore little off-white shell earrings and yellow ribbons in her hair.

He couldn't help the smile that split his face. Sometimes, quite out of the blue, he was stunned yet again by how beautiful she was.

"Hi," he said.

"Hi," she replied.

"I'm sorry," he said.

"You're sorry?" She seemed confused by this.

"Yes, I'm sorry," he said. "You're not ready for what I'm suggesting and I shouldn't have acted like a little boy about it. I'm sorry."

She still had that stunned look on her face. "Okay," she said.

"I love you," he told her, "and I will ask again, sometime. I hope you'll be ready then."

She just stared at him.

"If not, I'll give it time, ask again," he promised.

"I love you," he repeated.

She didn't say it back, but tears stood in her eyes and she hugged him, hard. He could feel her heart beating wildly against his chest, and momentarily worried that she might give herself a heart attack. Then he was chuckling at his own musings, and she pulled back to look at him suspiciously.

"You laughing at me?" she asked, looking a little like she might just kick his ass if he was.

"Not at all," he promised, still chuckling, and pulling her back to him.

She invited him in. Celia was out and Silvano was with Pamela in the other room. But they didn't do anything more than lie on her bed and cuddle. Well, at first he watched her strip off her dress and put on a soft-looking nightie thing, brush her hair and slip it into a scrunchy. Then they cuddled.

He feathered her bare shoulder with kisses; she played with the bit of skin at his elbow – an action she seemed to find comforting. It was peaceful.

He broke the silence with talk of his plans. "You know, for so long all I wanted was to make the West Indies team," he confessed. "I couldn't see beyond that at all. I didn't have a plan. I was like one of those cocky NBA draft hopefuls coming straight out of high school never doubting for a minute that he would get picked and shine at the highest level. The diamond ring and the whole nine yards. My injury caught me by surprise."

"Life does that," she said softly.

"Yeah, well even that didn't wake me up," he went on. "I didn't have a Plan B. And I just kinda drifted, not bothering to come up with one. Until now, at thirty, I don't have nothing to offer nobody."

She pulled away, turned around to peer down at him. "You think that's what this was about, what you have or don't have?" she demanded.

"No," he insisted. "That's not what I'm saying. Well, not exactly. What I'm saying is my life have to be about something, I have to be at bat in my own life. If I can't offer you a man who is about something, then what I really have to offer you?"

"You're about something," she said. "I see you with the girls. I see how much you love the game."

He pulled her back down. "Well, lately, waiting for the axe to fall, I feel like the game working me instead of the other way around. I need to figure out what I going do with the rest of my life. I can't keep waiting for somebody else to determine that. It just leave me feeling like less than a man."

20

Selena.

She wanted to tell him he was more man than any man she'd ever been with. Sure, he was a little lost, but he wasn't afraid to say so. And he wasn't afraid to come to her, to be the first to say I'm sorry, while she still was trying to figure out who was to blame. He was a different animal than any man she'd ever known.

Selena thought she must have dozed in his arms because the next thing she knew it was raining. Heavy drops on the galvanize roof beating out a rhythm.

"Looks like you're stuck here," she teased, hoping to lighten the mood.

"Until your sister sneaks in with her frying pan, anyway," he teased back.

"I don't think so; she been keeping some long nights lately. I do believe Celia might be seeing someone, which would explain why she's eased up somewhat on me about you," she said.

"Mmm ... this is one of my favourite sounds," he murmured.

"What is?"

"Raindrops on a galvanize roof."

"I like the smell of rain on grass," she said. "Actually, I like the fresh smell everything has after the rain."

"Well, that's relative," he said with a little chuckle. "When I was little, the house my mother and I lived in had an outside toilet. Like the rain used to just raise up the scent."

Selena smiled, thinking about *Tia*'s pit latrine.

"What you laughing at?" he asked.

"I was just thinking that between the two of us, we ought to be able to come up with a happy memory or two," she said, laughing more.

"We are kinda starting to sound a little like something out of *Oliver Twist* or *Angela's Ashes*," he murmured. "But I'll have you know I had a very fun childhood. Sometimes."

"Oh yeah?"

"Oh yeah," he said. "I had a pet chicken."

"A pet chicken."

"Yeah. It was black with streaks of red. Hurt. I nursed it, made it better after it got hurt," he said. "Of course, that backfired when its mother pecked it to death."

She slapped him hard in the chest, "Don't do that to me."

He laughed, "What? Okay, okay, you know what I remember about my childhood? Marking the passing of time by which fruit was in season," he said. "My favourite was mango season in early summer. Dumps season was good, too, and plum season. Guava season. But I had the best time during the summer, and climbing the mango trees with my friends – on somebody else's property, of course – was a ritual. You see this scar down my leg? I got that trying to hightail it over a wire fence with the owner of the land coming fast behind us, firing his gun in the air." He laughed at the shocked expression on her face.

"Then, of course, there was playing cricket after school, using everything from a coconut bough to a flat piece of wood as a bat," he continued. "Sometimes playing rounders with the girls. Kite flying in Easter. We used to make the kites out of either old plastic or newspaper with the spine from the coconut leaf making up the skeleton of the kite. Old rags and string as the tail. Turkleberry holding the whole thing together."

He ended on a little chuckle. "Is all of that happy enough for you?"

"I didn't play outside much," she confessed. "I was the strange, quiet one. You know, reading books, playing with my dolls. I remember I used to pretend they were real, real babies, you know. I loved babies. Wanted one of my own to love as far back as I can remember. I used to like going to church, too, before my mother stopped. I found the rituals calming, I guess."

"You were Catholic?"

"Yeah."

"Me too," Michael said. "I haven't been in a while. We have to go some time."

"That might be nice," she agreed.

"What else did you like?" Michael asked.

"I liked going to the beach," she said. "They're not like the beaches here. The beaches here are quiet by comparison. There it was like Carnival. I could sit back and people-watch, feast on all kinds of treats from the sour to the sweet. With so many tourists around, the vendors were out in full force. It had an energy you don't find on the beaches here.

"Of course, you have to drive a lot further to get there. I remember once we drove out to the beach with some cousins; on the way back we got caught in a traffic jam for hours. But it's not like the traffic jams on TV; everybody sweating and angry. It was like another kind of party; people liming, bodies hanging out of windows, music blasting."

"Party girl," he teased.

"I'm not," she insisted, "you know that. Just, sometimes, I like being around people, feeling them, observing them. And sometimes – okay, most times – I like my peace and quiet."

"I know that, too," he teased. "All them silent treatment you gave me in the beginning. Like, 'Why this man don't just go away and leave me in peace?'"

She blushed, laughed, thinking what a snob she'd been at first.

"I'd love to go there with you some time," he said, when they'd both sobered up a little.

She thought about that for a bit. "I'd like that, too," she finally said.

21

Michael.

His mother had been pretty once. He could see that, even if the pictures weren't there to tell the tale. But now her face was all stone, tight lips and pained eyes. She wore her suffering like a second skin. It made him ache to be around her sometimes, which was why, when he'd been a boy, Uncle Wellie's world had seemed such an oasis.

From the desert of her sadness to music, cricket, books, learning to swim at Fort, digging for cockles, roasting fish over a dug-out barbecue pit in the backyard, conversation, laughter. Sometimes he felt overwhelmed by the need to just hug her; to reach out, put his arms around her and take in her pain. Just take it away, so that he could see her body lose that stiffness. But when, as a boy coming up, he'd attempted contact, she'd only stiffened up. "Boy, come off me; you don't feel how it hot," she'd said, shrugging him off.

He sat at the table in the small kitchen looking at her now, her back to him as she spooned the Sunday standard of saltfish and antroba onto his plate before reaching into the oven for the toasted bread, then slicing off a piece of pear to complete the ensemble. He sipped at his cocoa, watching her, his heart clenching with a strange kind of pain, of yearning he couldn't quite put his finger on. All his life, he'd wanted to know her. All she'd ever allowed him, or anyone, to see was her hurt, her rejection, the burden of raising a child alone after being used up and tossed away. He wondered now what she thought about, if she thought about anything else at all.

"What you looking at me so for?" she asked. And he realized that he'd been caught staring.

"Nothing," he mumbled.

She gave him a long considering look before turning back to her plate and proceeded to eat standing over the sink, looking out through the back window.

"Mom, why you don't sit with me little bit?" he surprised himself by suggesting.

She seemed just as startled as he was. His mother never sat down to meals at the dining table. She sat in the living room in front of the television, stood at the counter, anywhere but around the table. When he was younger it had seemed normal enough. She often had so much to do; not sitting two minutes to eat a meal properly hadn't seemed out of place. But now, with her just standing and him mere feet away, sitting, it seemed silly.

He pulled out a chair for her.

"Junior, I don't have time for that," she began; "the chicken still have to season. I have to grate up the cheese for the macaroni pie."

"Arlene will help you with all that when she come home; just sit with me little bit," he insisted. And, surprisingly, she acquiesced, even favoured him with a little smile.

"Hm, the way you been running out of here lately, like fire under you foot, I didn't think you remember me, much less to sit down have breakfast with me," she said, her tone somewhere between a scold and a tease.

His answer, he supposed, could nudge it either way. They didn't exactly have a teasing relationship, though, so odds were it wouldn't need much help going the other way.

"What do you mean?" he mumbled.

"Junior, I look fooly to you?" she asked. He, of course, did not answer.

"From what I hear, this sound kind of serious," she continued. "Who this girl?"

So there it was, bold as you please, out in the open. He was scared. He knew how his mother felt about love and relationships; how she would see his actions as another rejection in a long line of many rejections. He was scared because he didn't want his love for Selena tainted by any of the drama in his mother's life and in their relationship.

"You sound like you know plenty already," he said, unable to keep the defensive tone out of his voice.

"Hey, you don't have to tell me nothing, you know," his mother began; "is not like you tell me your business anyway."

Michael sighed, "Look, Mom."

But she was not to be stopped. "I bet Uncle Wellie know. I bet your father people know, too. Asha, Tanty Lindo, all of them."

And he snapped. "Well, you're the one who wanted them to be a part of my life, right? So why lament about it now? Besides, it's not like I had any reason to think you'd be interested. It's not like you ever show any interest in who I might be seeing, apart from your little speech years and years ago about not trusting or letting people use me.

"Did you ever give me any reason to think you'd welcome the idea that I might be serious about someone?"

She looked hurt at this, and he regretted striking out. She got up heavily, put both their dishes in the sink. Then with her back turned, "So it serious then?"

"I love her," he replied.

"Love?" she sighed.

"Yes, love. It don't have to be a bad thing, you know."

She remained silent as she washed the dishes, and didn't turn to him again until she'd put them in the draining tray.

"So, I hear is some Spanish girl," she said.

"Her name is Selena. Selena Cruz."

She didn't ask if Antiguan girls weren't good enough for him any more, and for that he was grateful.

"You want to meet her?" he asked.

"Junior, is up to you," she said.

"No. It's up to you. You tell me if it's okay to bring her here. Because if I don't hear that from you, I am not going to bring her here. Because I don't want her to be hurt or embarrassed if I do."

She looked vaguely surprised at this.

"Yes," he said. "Remember Claudia, the Dominican girl I liked in high school? By the time you were done with your third degree on who she was and who her family was, she didn't want to have nothing to do with me again."

"What, I not supposed to ask questions?"

"And if is not that, is the cold freeze you give Bethann. Like she not even there."

"Please, that nothing girl! You can do better than that."

"Look! My point is, I'm not going to bring Selena here if you not going to treat her properly," he reiterated.

"So you going to tell me how to behave now? Don't forget who's the parent here and who's the child," she said.

"I am not a child. I'm a grown man. And I don't need your permission on this. All I'm asking for is a little courtesy."

"Well ..." she said.

"Well?" he enquired, not backing down either.

A long pause. "Well, bring her." And she turned and left the room, cutting off further conversation on the matter.

22

Selena.

She liked Michael's mother. She'd already felt like she understood her, and now meeting her, she found her spirit quite took to her. Sure, she was suspicious, but Selena read that it had less to do with her nationality than with his mother's concern over what was best for her son. She had a case of that affliction most mothers seemed to come down with: an inability to let go. Her own mother had proven to be the exception to that rule. But having given birth to her own child, she quite understood how strong that connection was; how much your children felt like a part of yourself; how unnatural the severing of their will from your own must seem.

The thing that convinced her about his mother was the way she took Silvano and smiled as she chatted with him. Seriously. Not that baby talk most people used. He frowned and seemed to meet her eyes as though considering her questions, his lips working as though yearning to give her an answer that was more than just meaningless blather. It made her smile.

She discovered that Michael's mother, who had worked as a nurse most of her life and was now semi-retired, working at the community clinic as midwife, also loved crocheting. So they discussed that a bit and promised to exchange patterns.

"Your mother's nice," she told him as he walked her home.

"That wasn't my mother," he responded with all seriousness. "That was some kind of pod person."

And she laughed.

23

Michael.

The new radio station, Wadadli Radio, asked him to do cricket reporting/commentary for the upcoming Test series.

Never having done any reporting before, he was taken by surprise. But it was an upstart radio station, and didn't want the same old voices, routine, and perspectives.

"Do it," Asha insisted.

"But what about my job?" he challenged.

"What about it?" she said. "I don't see what one have to do with the other."

"I don't see how I'll be able to keep it from them," he said. "It's radio."

"You committing a crime?" she demanded.

"No, but ..."

"But nothing ... boy, just do the thing," she said. "Is extra dollars, a new door. Besides, the way they laying off people these days it don't do to have all your eggs in that basket."

"Well, the series don't start for another month, so I guess I have time to figure out how to do this thing," he mused.

"What how? It's cricket. You know cricket. Just talk your piece. That's what they want you for, not your great reporting skills," she said.

"Still, I don't want to be no joke," he hit back. "Remember when Magic was doing commentary for basketball?"

She smiled at that. "Hm. That's true. I love Magic to death, but eloquent he's not," she agreed. "You handle yourself okay, though. Just relax, shoot straight, be yourself ... and try not to cut down the grammar tree."

"Thank you very much!"

She was laughing at the outraged look on his face. "What? I'm just saying," she said.

"Michael, come on, you'll be fine," she added a little bit later, more soberly, seeing that he was genuinely worried.

"So you going to Tanty Lindo for Christmas?" he asked a little later.

"I have a choice?" she shot back.

He hesitated some more, then, "I was thinking of bringing Selena."

"Well ...," she mused. "It'll certainly focus my mother's attention away from me."

"Very comforting, Asha."

"What? No. Look. Ent she already meet your mother? That didn't go bad. Who knows? Remember whatever happen, however they feel, the Lindo people not likely to make a scene."

"I don't want her to be uncomfortable."

"Please, uncomfortable!" she scoffed. "I've never felt comfortable at one of these things in my life. Besides, stop babying Selena; she can handle herself."

"And what would you know about it?"

"I know I never see you so – what's the word – solicitous before," Asha responded. "Like you 'fraid she goin' break. It would be cute if it wasn't so insulting and borderline sexist. I've been around Selena some, and she might look little and everything, but I can read people and I don't think she break all that easy. So, ease up."

Turned out he was the one feeling fragile at Tanty Lindo's annual family Christmas affair. He came in to find a strange, yet familiar, man sitting on the couch next to Tanty Lindo. For the pleasure of sitting next to this man, she'd given up what Michael liked to think of as her high chair. She had a gentle smile on her face. The man's eyes came up to meet his and his fingers tightened on Selena's arm.

"Michael?" she questioned.

He glanced over at Asha, who only shrugged, looking as surprised as he did.

"What?" Selena questioned.

He didn't answer, his eyes drawn back to the man who had sired him, and then run.

Michael felt frozen. He'd yearned to meet this man all his life. Had imagined it in moments of loneliness; moments of anger at his mother for some childhood injustice real or imagined; moments when he needed to talk or understand or feel like he belonged somewhere. And now the moment was here, and he felt frozen.

Asha nudged him a little. "Don't just stand up there with your mouth open; you goin' catch flies."

He forced his feet to move, moved with Selena to a corner of the room without having introduced her to anyone. No one noticed. There were enough distractions with Daniel Lindo home with his family for the first time in much too long. The room was full of laughter, and talk, rich with the smell of Christmas turkey and ham, fruit cake, and various blended scents. Nat King Cole sang "The Christmas Song", Tanty Lindo's favourite.

Michael stood propped up against the wall feeling hot and sticky and slightly nauseous, Selena eyeing him worriedly.

"Michael, what's the matter?" she asked.

He didn't speak right away, simply inclined his head to the pair on the couch. The man had stopped staring, was busy talking to his mother again, glancing up every few seconds or so to seek out the boy who looked so much like him.

"My father," he said.

"Your father?" she echoed, now staring herself.

He didn't answer and for a long time she didn't speak either. Then, "What are you going to do?"

He shrugged.

Asha came over then. "The two of you-all look like you-all see ghost," she said. "Snap out of it. Is only a human being, Michael, and I doubt he worth all this."

When he didn't answer, she grabbed Selena's elbow. "Come, Selena, let me introduce you around since Michael don't seem up to the task just now."

Selena was not given a chance to respond and soon found herself dragged into the sea of Lindos. Michael was regretful about abandoning her to his class-conscious cousins, aunts and uncles, but grateful for the moment to himself.

He slipped out of a side door to the house's wrap-around porch. As a child, it had been one of his favourite spots, the pillars all around embraced by running plants. The plants now had dominance, were a part of the pillars which had split to accommodate them. From some parts of the porch you couldn't even see the skies or the cars passing, so dense was the foliage.

He had been standing, sitting, occasionally pacing in one such area for he didn't know how long when he heard a voice behind him.

"So, you're Delora's son," the voice stated.

"Yours too," Michael said, not turning to meet it.

The man drew closer. He cleared his throat. "So, how is Delora?" he asked.

"Bitter and angry."

"Not after all this time?"

And Michael turned then, something fierce stirring inside him though he did not raise his voice. It hissed out of him. "Why not after all this time?"

The man stepped back as though from a blow. Michael turned away, digging his hands into his pockets, breathing heavily, feeling hot and sweaty again.

He knew his father hadn't left, could still feel him there. But he didn't speak, not for a long time.

"Looks like she did okay with you," Daniel Lindo said lamely. "I heard about when you made the West Indies team. I was so proud. I know you didn't get that athletic skill from my side. I was never much of a sportsman. I work in entertainment management. Have my own company. I was always more of a negotiator, people manager. If I'd stayed here I might've ended up a politician."

He chuckled a little at this, then continued his soft murmuring. "I didn't want to stay here. I didn't feel like I could be my own person here. I love Mammy to death, but she live on this other planet, boy. There's no having personal will around her.

"She wasn't happy with me when I left. But not for the reason you might think. No, she didn't want me settling down with child and wife just then, especially not somebody she didn't approve of. But she didn't see why I had to go all the way to Canada to become, as she put it, a little fish in a big pond. I had the chance to be somebody, didn't have to run all the way to Canada because some 'nothing girl' claimed she was wi' chile for me. Her words.

"The truth is, I was running from her, from her expectations, her demands. I was just happy for the excuse. I look at this house falling down around her and I know I would've felt suffocated in her world. I ran because I wanted my own life, not just because I was scared of being a father, though that truthfully did feel like

another noose. But it was an excuse. A good one. But an excuse."
Michael stood there, feeling like somebody was beating him over
the shoulders with a hard, fresh piece of bull-bud.

The man whose name he'd been given seemed to awaken from
his musings. "I guess the time for explanations and all that long
past. Tell Delora ... tell her ... tell her Merry Christmas."

Then he was gone.

Michael heard the door open and close behind him, laughter
and talk spilling out before being suddenly cut off. He stood there
longer still remembering once, in primary school, when their mid-
morning play had been interrupted by a heavy-set woman strid-
ing up through the playground and up the stairs to Sister's office,
her son in tow.

Michael was hard pressed to remember the boy's name now, but
he recalled him being a bit of a smartass, one of the older kids who
didn't have much time or patience with those his age. He remembered the entire playground frozen in silence as blows from the
thick leather belt the woman had brought in the brown paper
bag fell on the boy's narrow shoulders again and again, while
Sister stood watching and nodding her approval. Corporal pun-
ishment was something they were used to at the Catholic school,
but this was something else altogether, a throwback to one of
those 100-stripe whippings with the cat-o-nine they learned
about in history class.

The boy didn't cry, and when she was done the woman walked
down the steps and out the yard as purposefully as she had
entered. Sister went back to her office.

The boy came down the steps to the yard, and shortly after that
the bell rang.

Michael never forgot that incident, or how beaten the boy
seemed every day he saw him after that. He didn't tease the
younger boys any more. He didn't have that poor-boast walk fifth
graders, trying to impress sixth-grade girls, adopted. He was just
there, and wasn't at the same time. Something had been beaten
out of him, something of his spirit knocked out by that big, thick
belt and his mother's hefty arms and the stares of his peers and the
gleam in Sister's eyes.

Years later, Michael remembered seeing him on a prison gang.
His eyes had a dead look to them.

Michael felt, in the wake of his conversation with his father, the way that boy had looked after that momentous public beating. And, like the boy, he didn't cry.

24

Selena.

He never came back inside, never ate anything. But Selena didn't have time to feel out of place with Asha claiming her and dragging her here and there.

She made up a plate for him, took it out when Asha finally gave her some breathing room.

He didn't take it, simply said, "You ready? I'm leaving."

He wouldn't get any argument from her. This wasn't exactly her crowd. Besides, she could see he was hurting. It was there in the harshness of his tone, and the stiff way he held himself. She'd noticed this before. Men didn't seem to know what to do with their pain. The women she knew moved through it, past it. Men seemed to fight it. But she knew this; it had to come. There was no fighting it. You just made it harder for yourself when you struggled against it.

She went with him. They didn't even tell anybody they were leaving, just walked out to the road and walked some more until a driver took pity on them. Buses weren't exactly plentiful on Christmas Day and never ran in this area.

He walked her home from town where their ride let them off.

"You want to go somewhere and talk?" she asked. Pamela and Silvano weren't home. The two had gone to the Dominican Republic for Christmas. But Celia might be around or she would've invited him in.

In any case, he just shook his head, something lost in his eyes.

She hugged him then, reaching up to peck his lips. "It doesn't matter about him," she whispered. "He's not nearly the man you are. Forget behind; just look forward." Then she released him. He turned to go, his feet heavy, his thoughts turned inward. She stood on the steps watching and worrying until he disappeared.

Then walked into a nightmare of her own.

Celia was there. And so was Victor; the two of them sitting worriedly in the kitchen. Victor was gulping a glass of water.

"Selena," Celia said with a start.

"Silvano's not here," Selena directed at Victor, not in the mood for him at the moment. "He's gone to see his grandmother. With no help from you. What you doing here? You have a Christmas present for him?"

Victor didn't speak.

"Selena, we have a problem," Celia said.

"Problem? What problem?" she asked, still distracted by her worry about Michael and annoyed at Victor's presence.

"Victor's in trouble," Celia said. "See, he was working this job leading up to the holidays. The labour office came down on them a couple of days ago. You know they've been keeping an eye on the sub-contractor he gets most of his jobs from, and they busted a whole bunch of them for working without permits. You know he doesn't work steady: don't have a permit. So he was held, too. Police and labour officers were taking them in and he got frightened. He pushed down one of the officers and ran away. That was the day before Christmas Eve. It was in the paper. Police now looking for him. Likely they going to send him home. Now, he might be charged for assault, resisting arrest, though he really wasn't under arrest."

Selena just stared at the two of them like they were crazy. She felt like she'd walked into a movie.

"What?" she asked, dazed. "And he came here?"

"I told him it was okay," Celia said.

"Okay? Okay? How can that be okay? What are we supposed to do with all this trouble?" Selena demanded, her voice rising with each word.

"Look, we can't just abandon him," Celia insisted. "With times getting hard, they're cracking down on foreigners. Just the other day Baby Doll – you know Marilu's housemate, the Jamaican girl – she got sent home. Now that girl wasn't taking a thing out of nobody mouth; peace to the dead, as they say. You have to know she was a saint if she and Marilu could live together as good as they did. Yet, they picked on her. What you think they're going to do with Victor?"

"Celia, you take leave of your senses? The man hit a policeman," Selena said.

"Not hit, push; and it wasn't a policeman. It was one of the labour officers," Celia argued.

The sisters' eyes met at that, and the stand-off stretched, Victor uncharacteristically silent.

Finally, it was Celia who blinked. She sighed, "Look, Sel, he just need a place ..."

But Selena was already shaking her head, "No."

"Selena ..."

"No."

"Look, this is my place. He can stay if I want him to."

Selena looked and felt like she'd been slapped, but pressed on, having had about enough of her sister's championing of this man who had hurt her so much.

"Celia, you do what you need to do," she said. "Kick out your sister for a man if that's what you feel you need to do."

"Kick out? Who said anything about kicking anybody out?" Celia asked, baffled.

"I am not staying in the same house with him ever again," Selena said, spelling out each word. "I made that clear a long time ago. You choose to throw the fact that this is your place in my face so you can keep him here. Fine. You've made your choice."

"You want him back home catching hell?" Celia demanded. "Is that what you want? Or worse, in jail? Will that pay you back for everything? Will that make anything okay? What's wrong with you?"

"What's wrong with me? What's wrong with you? I would never put anything before my sisters. And certainly not a man who had hurt one of them as much as he hurt me. You know, I have to wonder what's the story with you and him. What *is* the story with you and him? You want him; is that it?"

She paused at this, then, "Or maybe you have him already. After all, I know from experience what he can do in the bedroom, how it can mess with your head enough. It took one blow too many to my head to clear up the fog."

Celia's eyes flickered away, and that gave Selena her answer. She sat heavily at the same table across from Victor, who seemed almost to be trying to blend into the furniture. She sat because she suddenly felt wrung out and weak-kneed all at once.

Celia loudly pulled up a chair close to hers, took her hand. "Selena, I'm not trying to hurt you," Celia said. "But you never could let go of things and move on. Victor made mistakes, like all of us ..."

Selena took back her hand, stood. "Celia, I don't want to hear about Victor from you." Then quieter still, "I don't want to hear this shit from you."

She went to her room, threw her clothes into a bag, hastily packed what remained at the house of Silvano's stuff. Altogether it wasn't much. Though it made quick work of things, that fact made her sadder still. There was a pain in her stomach like someone had kicked her there, hard. Her heart beat like it wanted to break through her chest; confrontations of any kind always did that to her.

And though a little part of her hoped, her sister never came to the room. She could still hear them talking, moving around.

It was only when she stepped outside and the cool wind hit the water on her face that she realized she'd been crying. And it was only then it really hit her that she had nowhere to go.

She didn't have friends or family in Antigua. Only Michael and, in a limited way, his circle of friends. There was nothing here that was her own.

She fought against just sinking to the steps, and waiting for life to figure it out. She went to the only friend she did have in Antigua, Michael, the man whose invitation to live together she had previously turned down.

He wasn't there. It was his mother who responded to her knocking, and invited her in, and told her he hadn't yet come home, and asked her if she was okay. And held her as she finally put her bags and her troubles down and let it go for a while. This woman, who Michael insisted didn't know how to be anything but bitter and off-putting, made her feel warm again; and she hadn't thought that was possible.

25

Michael.

He didn't feel like going home, being alone with his thoughts. Didn't feel like talking about it, which he would have to do if he went to Uncle Wellie's or back to Selena's.

He ended up at Deeno's. His friend usually had a good Christmas lime going, and this year was no exception. He heard the music from halfway up the road, could see the crowd spilling out from Deeno's yard into the street.

He headed straight for the cooler before he even spotted his friend, had gulped half of his beer before he felt Deeno slap him on the back.

"You made it," Deeno said.

"Yeah, yeah," he mumbled.

"So, where your other half?"

"Home."

"It's just as well," Deeno said.

"What you mean by that?" he asked.

"Guess who here."

"Deeno, man, I not in the mood for games; either tell me or don't tell me," he snapped.

"But eh-eh, a what happen to you?" Deeno demanded. "What make you so surly, this big Christmas?"

He didn't answer. "Who's here?" he asked, changing the subject.

"Old flames burn bright," his friend said cryptically before disappearing back into the crowd. Michael watched his friend's retreating back, annoyed, then shrugged, reaching for another beer.

"Go easy," a voice behind him warned. He stood, turned, to find Bethann way within his personal space. He had to admit she was looking good, still one of the sexiest women he knew with her almost blue-black skin, long dark hair, long, thick lashes, and sensuous curves that always reminded him of one of Uncle Wellie's sculptures.

"Bethann," he greeted.

She kissed him on the lips before he could react to stop her, "Merry Christmas," she said, flashing perfect teeth.

And who could stay mad at Bethann? She was as bold and presumptuous as ever. "Merry Christmas," he greeted back, before stepping out of her personal space.

He danced with her quite a bit that night through a blitz of calypso tunes, losing his worries in the pulsing beat and the heady feel of her body pressed up against his, teasing.

When he wasn't dancing, he was drinking, like a man possessed, searching for that buzz: that high where your body tingled and your mind felt giddy. It wasn't as easy a thing to achieve as people thought. Underestimate, and you just ended up feeling deflated and bloated, making repeated trips behind some tree to empty your bladder. Overestimate, and you skipped the high altogether, falling off the precipice to drunkenness and a hangover, neither of which he particularly enjoyed.

"I think you've had just about enough," Bethann said, taking his latest bottle of beer from his hand. He looked at her, then leaned heavily against the house dry-washing his face with his hand. "What's the matter with you, eh, Michael?" she asked.

He stared bleakly at her face, her pretty face, feeling lost and slightly out of focus. He felt like he was trying, without luck, to grab onto his thoughts.

She took his hand. "Come on," she said, "let's get out of here."

And he followed her.

26

Selena.

In the morning, she sat at the table with his mother, drinking tea. "So what you goin' to do?" Michael's mother asked, gently.

Selena shrugged. "I don't know," she replied, finally. "I just don't even want to deal with my sister right now. The only thing I want to do, the only thing I want to do is hold my baby."

She laughed dryly, adding, "But of course he's all the way home, in the Dominican Republic."

Just then, the front door opened and Michael stumbled in. She'd been aware, of course, that he hadn't come home the previous night; had been worried about him on top of her own worry.

He looked bad, wrung out. She wanted to hold him, but restrained herself. And he was actually the first to speak.

"Selena, what you doing here?"

His mother got up then, took the now empty cups over to the sink.

She said the first thing that popped into her head: "I think I might need to go home for a while."

She couldn't read his reaction. He was startled, a bit taken aback, hurt … and guilty? She rushed to allay his worries. "It's not about us," she explained. "It's just … look, I know things are rough with you right now … but I need to be with my child right away."

"Something happen?" he asked.

And she felt her eyes fill with tears, thinking of the rift between her and her sister. Her sisters had been a constant in her life. Through their disagreements, and the upheavals that came with their father leaving and mother remarrying, they'd had each other. Now, her sister was not only harbouring but, from all indications, was more deeply involved than she'd ever realized with the man who'd hurt her more than any other. She couldn't seem to wrap her mind around that.

Selena knew Celia defended Victor. She knew that her sister disliked Michael, but had thought it merely her prejudice against Antiguans and darker skinned ones at that. To discover that there was so much more that she hadn't read felt like the deepest betrayal. She didn't know how to forgive what Celia had done. Worse, her sister seemed more caught up with saving this man than with salvaging their relationship. She hadn't tried to stop her from leaving, had she?

She leaned heavily into Michael and she cried.

"Well, this has been a memorable Christmas," she joked weakly when she could talk again.

"You want to talk about what happened?" he asked.

She shrugged. "How are you doing?" she asked.

He laughed, a little bitterly. "It's been some Christmas."

She touched his face wishing he could share this pain with her. "Look, I'm sorry I pulled away like that yesterday," he said. "I just needed time to process things."

"And have you?" she asked.

"Well, before I had no father and a stupid kind of childish hope in something – I don't know what. Now, I have neither. And it's just as well. Because neither was very good for me. I'm not the first child to grow up without a father. No reason why it has to be the defining thing in my life," he said, not as convincingly as she was sure he would've liked.

She kissed his cheek where her palm had been, found herself suddenly fighting the sudden overwhelming urge to jump him right there. She knew in a part of her mind that there was nothing good or purely passionate about it; that it was driven by some kind of primal need to erase both their pain by sinking into their most basic form of pleasure; to connect.

"Let me come with you," he said suddenly. And she looked at him like he was crazy, feeling like she'd missed part of the conversation somehow. "Come with me where?"

"Home," he said. "I think I need to get away for a bit, too."

"You can't," she reminded him. "You have a job, remember? And you're supposed to be doing that commentating thing soon."

"I can get time from work," he insisted. "It's not like I've ever used any of my vacation time. And 'that commentating thing' is not until late January. I have time. And I want to be with you."

She thought about it and couldn't come up with a good reason to say no, so she didn't. She smiled, and said, "Well, we'll have to stay with my *tia*. I think there's quite enough people at *Mami*'s house."

27

Michael.

The Dominican Republic was nothing like he'd expected. It was hot, flooded with people, crazy traffic, and he felt totally swallowed up in a language and culture he didn't understand.

Selena's aunt smiled at him a lot and was constantly trying to get him to eat. The aunt was a lot darker than Selena, closer to his own complexion. Her home was simple, in a busy residential area with lots of children. He had to dip up water from the cistern under the verandah for bathing, and the toilet was a pit like he'd had at home when he was little. But everything was clean, and with the Jesus clock, Mary statue, straw cross, and family pictures across the cabinet, it wasn't that different from his mother's house. Selena's aunt was warm; that was the only word he could think of to describe her.

Selena's mother was a lot more watchful. Never blatantly rude, but a little unsure about him. He suspected she would have been the same about any man for her daughter, especially after Victor.

One of his more interesting moments involved her. Selena had gone out with some friends, and after a day trekking from one tourist site to the next he'd felt seriously drained and had begged off, offering to stay and keep an eye on the baby so that Pamela could go too. It was her first outing to a club, and one of her favourite local bands was playing, so he knew she'd appreciate it.

He sat watching the television, though he didn't understand a thing being said, with Silvano sitting sleepily in his lap. It had been a long day for the child, too. Selena's mother brought him some coffee. He liked the coffee here. It was like a shot of some good rum. It went straight to your head, opened your eyes, warmed your skin. To compare that to the coffee he usually drank at home was like trying to compare American beer to German beer. No comparison.

She sat down. Her husband was already sleeping, which, come to think of it, was the only time he ever saw her still. As long as there were people around and, in particular, her husband and the boys, she was constantly on the go. Consequently, she was young and fit; looked more like an older sister to Selena than a mother.

She said something to him that he didn't understand. His high-school Spanish couldn't keep up with her rapid-fire speech. Hell, to tell the truth, he couldn't even keep up when she talked really slowly, like he was stupid. Just that morning's incident, when he tried to get her to understand that he needed to borrow an iron, complete with pantomime, was evidence of that. Still, she tried.

He looked a question at her, and she repeated her comment, slower this time. Still, all he caught was *los tres ojos*. He'd been there just that afternoon with Selena. It was a beautiful natural tourist spot consisting of caves, with the still waters inside glistening off the walls, and the significantly lower temperature providing a respite from the heat outside.

He nodded and smiled, repeated after her, "*Los tres ojos.*"

She nodded, "*Bueno?*"

"*Bueno,*" he agreed.

She asked another question. The only thing he picked out was "*mañana*" and "Puerto Plata."

He knew they were supposed to be going to Puerto Plata later that week to visit the beach and for Selena to catch up with an old friend. "*Non,*" he said, "*non mañana. Ah … ah … Sábado.*"

She smiled, nodded. He didn't know how to explain that they had plans to go shopping tomorrow, so he left well enough alone.

But she didn't. "You love Selena?"

That he understood. "*Yes,*" he said, nodding emphatically. "*Sí.*"

She nodded, too, touched his chest where his heart rested, then took his hand and stared him down hard. That he understood, too.

"I'll be good to her," he said in his own tongue, not sure how else to get it across. But she nodded, understood.

The day at the beach was fun. That was the other memory that would stay with him. There were a lot of people there too; a lot of food; a lot – almost too much – of everything. But Selena was freer here than he'd ever seen her; and he liked seeing her laugh with her friends and talk like the words were running away and she had to keep up with them.

He liked her in that golden yellow one-piece lycra number he'd bought for her when they went shopping. Good luck trying to get her to wear something like that in Antigua. Here, it was like she shed her inhibitions. And he went with the flow of that until, a little tipsy himself on *Presidente,* he found himself making out with her as discreetly as one could in a little private spot in the crowded waters with children splashing nearby.

He dipped his hand beneath the lycra suit, caressing her under the cover of the water until her breath quickened. He loved being this illicit with her.

"You're so different here," he whispered in her ear.

"I can be me here," she breathed back.

And he understood. In Antigua, it was so important to her not to fit into the stupid stereotypes that she guarded herself closely, not wanting to be pigeon-holed as this or that. Here, she didn't have to worry, especially out here on the beach where she didn't have to deal with her mother, her family or any of her troubles.

He knew she and her mother had argued about the rift between her and Celia. She'd told him what had happened, and he understood why she'd been shaken by it. Her sisters were home to her; more so than this country or her mother or anything. She'd thought their bond – the differences of opinion notwithstanding – unshakeable. She'd been wrong. But out here, under the sun in the cooling waters, she seemed to put even the pain of that down.

He remembered their first trip to the beach; how that had been the beginning of her opening to him.

It aroused him further. They couldn't do very much out in plain sight like this. But he enjoyed just touching her, making her feel. It was so rare to see her just let herself go. It was almost as though she were afraid to feel, sometimes, afraid of her body.

He loved her during sex, when he unlocked something inside and she became all sensation, forgetting to be self-conscious or tentative or afraid. He remembered one of their little fights about that bit of analysis.

He liked watching her, had been watching her. And she grew uncomfortable under his gaze, asked him to stop. He'd observed, "You're very self-conscious."

"Stop that!" she'd snapped.

"What?"

"Stop analysing me," she'd demanded. "Stop trying to climb into my head."

"Maybe I want to climb in your head," he'd teased.

And she'd pulled back from him a little, gathering herself. "I don't like that," she said. "I don't like people trying to dissect me."

And he'd pushed a little more. "Well, sometimes you don't give me no choice. I ask what you thinking, is always the same answer – 'Nothing.' I ask what you feeling; you shrug. You so uptight sometimes. It make me want to climb in and figure you out. Sometimes I can't even figure if you here with me or not, if you want me here or not. How you feel. Nothing."

How ironic that he'd been the one to pull back inside himself the day his dreams of his father had crumbled. She'd been the one to reach out, and he'd gone and done something he still didn't want to think about. If relief from the pain was what he'd needed, why hadn't it been with her?

He didn't get that.

She chose that moment to turn around in his arms, and kiss him lightly on the lips. "*Te amo,*" she said.

28

Selena.

He went home at the start of the third week. They made love the night before he left, which wasn't easy in *tia's* house, but they managed it. The aunt must've known, but she didn't say anything. She'd been a lot more accepting of the whole relationship than Selena's mother.

But, of course, her mother was also worried about Celia. They'd fought about that. Sisters didn't turn their backs on sisters over men, she'd said. And Selena had wanted to snipe back: 'No, only mothers do.' Naturally, she hadn't. And of course Selena agreed, which is why what Celia had done had hurt so much.

She had no idea how Celia had solved her little dilemma, but assumed she'd find out when she returned. Would serve her right to get deported alongside him for harbouring a fugitive, she thought meanly. But then her guilt, concern, and confusion overtook her again. She was worried, she could admit that. But she was also hurt, and right now hurt was winning.

So she accused her mother of never supporting her, of always taking Celia's side in things, of always giving men too much rope. That must be where Celia got it from, putting a philanderer and woman-beater ahead of her sister, she challenged.

These things had hurt her mother, she knew, but it didn't keep her from being civil to Michael or from watching the baby while they went on their excursions.

And playing tourist with Michael, Selena could pretend for a little while, holding his hand as they strolled through the halls of *Colombos's Alcazar* admiring this artifact or that, that everything was okay.

She had to leave soon. Pamela had to go back to school. The term had already started. But she didn't want to go. Selena suggested sending her sister back with Michael, but her mother wouldn't hear of it, and since they didn't know what was happening with Celia, her mother wasn't about to send her youngest daughter back into uncertainty.

So the pressure was on Selena to make up her mind, and quickly, though she, too, likely didn't have a job or a place to stay. She'd left so suddenly, Cecil hadn't been happy. He told her Christmas wasn't a good time for her to be taking off; told her if she left against his wishes not to bother coming back.

Michael couldn't wait any longer. He had to return for that "commentary thing." He said he'd look for a place so she'd have somewhere to go when she came back. Though he insisted she could stay with him, she didn't want that. Running during a crisis into a situation she knew neither of them was ready for at the best of times was hardly a good idea.

She told him she'd be back soon. And she would, too. Pamela was already in a mood, anxious to get back to her life. So she had another sister not talking to her.

"You can't run forever," her aunt, who hardly ever interfered, said finally, a week after Michael left. Selena had been pensive. He'd called her just that day at her mother's place to report that he'd found her a place and that she even had a job to pay for it. Asha was doing a mural at Joey's, a popular restaurant on Fort Beach, and had told him they were looking for a hostess. Someone to look pretty and meet diners and coordinate the service staff. Asha could pull some strings.

He'd tried to smooth things over with Cecil, explain that she'd had a family emergency, but he was still upset about being left high and dry during the busy season, even if she was the best employee he'd ever had.

No, he hadn't found out anything about Celia. The few times he'd passed by the house, it had been closed up.

She didn't answer her *tia* right away; she had run out of excuses, she supposed. She had options now. Plus, Pamela had opportunities there that meant a lot to her, and she had a man she loved – something from which it would not be easy to walk away. That love had grown when he decided to come home with her, and he'd just fit into her life, ignoring the tensions and going with the flow. All this while he was still dealing with the emotional fall-out from his Christmas confrontation with his father.

It was time to get on with things.

29

Michael.

He really enjoyed commentating. He'd been nervous at first but found he had a knack for it. He knew his stuff, thanks primarily to his informal tutelage under Uncle Wellie.

"What did I tell you?" Asha asked.

"You were right, as always," he said.

She appraised him, sensing that the conversation had moved to deeper ground.

"I didn't want to be right about that," she said. "I guess I just know us Lindos too well. We're emotionally bereft. Or hadn't you noticed?"

He just stared at her.

"I mean, there's a reason I've never been able to make a relationship work, you know. Intimacy issues and all that," she plunged on.

"Stop feeling sorry for yourself," he said. "I'm the one who got dumped on, remember?"

He watched her bite back an instinctive response.

"Shit, Ash, I'm sorry," he apologized.

"No big deal," she said. "I was making it about me. And it's not. Look, Michael, he's a jerk. In my head, yes, he's always been for walking away from his kid. So now you know it, too. You don't need him. You never did."

He sucked his teeth, "I know I don't need him. I wanted him. Or I wanted him to be real or something. I don't know what I wanted. I just know that I didn't find it, and now I know I never will."

"Forget him!" she said.

"Yeah," he sighed, "forget him."

She opened a bottle of wine, and they finished the bottle, and under its influence he confessed his sin. "I slept with Bethann."

"Huh?" she asked, a little out of it, too, though truth be told she could always hold her liquor better than he.

"I slept with …"

"I heard you," she cut in.

"It happened that same night, after my little chat with daddy. Selena tried to get me to talk about it, but I found I couldn't. It was too fresh, too raw or something. I went to Deeno's party; Bethann was there. I ended up back at her place. She doesn't live with her mother any more. She has a really nice place, one of those housing developments out in Cedar Grove ..."

"What are you, selling me real estate?" she cut in again. "I don't care where she lives. What the hell possessed you? I thought you were in love."

"I am."

"And that's how you show it?" she demanded. "I tell you: men. You-all so damn predictable, it's not funny."

And he had no defence.

"She know?" she asked finally.

"You crazy?" he demanded.

"I don't think my sanity is the one in question here," she said. "You're the one screwing up a good thing, for what you, yourself, admitted a long time ago was a cheap screw. I guess you are a Lindo after all. You have to find a way to mess up a good thing."

"I thought you didn't like Selena," he challenged.

"Fine! Make this about me and my alleged dislike for Selena," she said. "I've been in enough relationships to recognize deflecting when I see it, in case you didn't know."

"Look, Asha, I was drunk, it happened. I don't have no excuse," he said.

"Michael, shut up," she said, drily. "Now you just sound like a stupid soap opera cliché. All we need now to complete the illusion is Selena eavesdropping behind the door. Too bad she's still in Santo Domingo, eh."

And with that she got up, went to her room, closing the door firmly behind her and leaving him to his thoughts. He escaped them in a drink-induced sleep, his long legs hanging over the edge of the couch.

30

Selena.

She didn't like the new job as much, though it paid more. It required too much smiling, too much talking, too much interaction with people she'd rather avoid. Seemed Joey's was a popular hangout for high-ranking government officials and businessmen. Big bellies, booming voices and laughter, and way too much familiarity for her comfort.

And she had to dress up more than she usually would; not the regular black-and-white waitress get-up. Joey, her new boss, provided an allowance, and Asha took her shopping, bringing some colour and a bit of cleavage into her wardrobe.

Michael did a double-take the first time he saw her. It wasn't over the top. She was working, after all. She had decided to stick with reds and yellows; the latter because it was her favourite colour, the former because Asha insisted that it was festive. So she got a pair of yellow tops, a pair of reds, and mixed and matched.

Since Joey hadn't insisted on a particular style for his hostess, Asha decided that the skirt should "move," and that the blouse should "fall a little bit, but not too much" off the shoulder. Selena found she always looked like she was heading to a party, which Asha insisted was the point.

Michael was turned on by the look.

"You don't think it's too much?" she worried, pulling the blouse up a little bit.

"What Joey say?"

"You've never met Joey, have you?" she asked. "Well, he's this very big, very expressionless man. He could fit in easily with the Mafia, I think. He just kind of grunted that it was fine. I really don't think he cares as long as I look pretty, act professional, and make the guests happy."

"Well, you do look pretty, and you're making me very happy," he teased.

And she smiled, because it was good to see him playful and happy, and to feel that way herself when it seemed so much was weighing on both of them lately.

He stripped the clothes off, and together they christened the new bed she'd be paying for for the next four or so years.

Michael came by Joey's sometimes during happy hour; sometimes by himself, sometimes with Deeno or Asha.

There was a little bit of tension between him and his cousin, but Selena dismissed it, having come to accept that those two, as close as they were, were always arguing about something.

A bit like her and Celia, she reflected. Celia had left the island, on Victor's heels apparently. According to Mariluz, they'd both taken off, reportedly for one of the Virgin Islands. Even her sister's best friend didn't know the details.

Mariluz confessed that Celia had been in love and involved with Victor for a while but hadn't told her. He'd been the one to encourage her in the cleaning business that never got off the ground. They were actually kind of good for each other, her sister's friend began, before biting her tongue, remembering to whom she was talking.

The new place was good enough, basically in the same neighbourhood. And she'd been able to retrieve whatever of their things had been left behind from their former landlady, who'd been glad to get rid of them.

Pamela was a little more subdued than usual, busy trying to catch up on the time she'd missed in school. In her spare time, she went to team practice, crocheted, read. They didn't have a television any more; that had been one of the items the landlady claimed hadn't been left behind during her sister's hasty flight. Asha loaned them her old radio, and Selena found herself listening to cricket sometimes to hear Michael's voice.

They were both so busy these days, him off island sometimes, that they didn't see as much of each other, though having her own place should have made things easier.

She thought they were okay, though. He came down for happy hour as often as he could, sometimes acting all jealous over the attention of some of the restaurant's patrons. She acted annoyed, but was secretly pleased. He stayed over some nights, but she found that often they were so tired, they just slept. And sleeping together was nice. They didn't necessarily cuddle through the night. Michael carried way too much heat when he was sleeping for that. But it felt good to have him there, even if he did snore. And she didn't think it was just because she was used to sharing a bed; had shared one all her life.

It was him, the reassuring familiarity of him in her life. It felt … nice.

31

Michael.

He liked the radio gig. He found that as Asha had assured him, he had a knack for it. They kept him on after the series to do a new show called Sports Action Line, which was made up of interviews with sports personalities, commentary by sporting pundits, and feedback from the public. He felt energized by the weekly programme, and it had become so popular they were talking about making it a daily.

It almost made up for the fact that his female cricket programme had been cut because of no funds and little public interest. That was the reason that was given, anyway. He had tried to hustle up some sponsorship to continue privately, but times were rough, what with the government's new tax measures and the worldwide recession.

He knew from the perspective of his bosses there was a lot more going on behind the scenes. And, as he'd confessed to Uncle Wellie, with the talk of retrenching workers, his second gig might be all the excuse they felt they needed to axe him.

"So leave," Uncle Wellie said.

"I can't," he said.

"Why not?"

"Because I like working with young people. The radio thing is fun, but it don't give me that. I have to keep active."

"You don't need them for that," Uncle Wellie insisted. "You still active in league cricket. You can try and build up a youth programme that way. You don't need no money; just start with the young people that interested and build up from there."

But he was scared. He knew he wasn't happy where he was, but he couldn't seem to get past the fear of stumbling backward to move forward. It was a classic case of knowing what you have but not knowing what you're going into.

"Well, sit down there and let them take the power to choose from you," Uncle Wellie had said finally, dismissively.

He spoke to Selena, maybe subconsciously hoping that her practical nature would validate his decision or lack of one. But she surprised him.

"I think you should do what makes you happy," she said. "That job not making you happy. You sound alive on radio."

"And what you know 'bout our sports?"

"I'm not stupid, Michael," she said, swatting him. "Besides, I might not know cricket or who Ridley ... Ambrose is ..."

"Curtley Ambrose. Ridley Jacobs," he corrected.

"Like I said, I may not know who they are, but I know you," she insisted. "And I know how crushed you and Pamela were when they cut your programme.

"I remember you saying it was just somebody with too much power being vindictive, perhaps because they thought you were getting too much ahead of yourself – a never-was, almost-been could've-been West Indies great from nowhere. You remember saying all that? These people at the station, on the other hand, seem to respect you and what you bringing. And, like I said, I know you, and it's a different you on radio than the one dragging out of here in the morning to go to work."

He smiled at that: at the fact that he was dragging out of there most mornings; that they were practically living together despite their decision all those months ago that they weren't ready for that. Selena seemed okay with taking the steps if they weren't held up for scrutiny beforehand. He smiled, too, at her acknowledgment; at the truth in her confident statement that she did know him. He smiled thinking how far they'd come. And warmed by everything he had with her, even in the face of all they'd both lost recently, he did feel like he could face his fear of the unknown.

He didn't walk in to work and quit the next day, but he did start to seriously consider it. He started talking seriously to the radio station about a daily programme and the kind of compensation he would need. He started talking seriously to the team with whom he played community cricket about doing a youth camp the following summer, and maybe beginning to work with interested young men and young women after that.

It would be like the steelbands had done, starting their various schools of pan after the death of panorama during the annual Carnival festivities.

He felt hopeful again.

32

Selena.

The tension on her new job was building. The waitresses resented her because she was not Antiguan, yet, as hostess, had some authority over them. One, in particular, refused to take orders from her. She was never so bold as to say, "Go to hell; don't tell me what to do." But she pretended not to hear whenever Selena spoke. Never looked directly at her; never responded directly to her. It figured that she would be the one most in need of discipline.

Hyacinth, the worker in revolt, was chronically late. Selena tried to talk gently to her about it, but the woman never acknowledged her; and when Selena did bite the bullet and talk to Joey about it, Hyacinth got worse.

His size and demeanor notwithstanding, Joey wasn't terribly aggressive, and Hyacinth was. He did try to talk to her, but it seemed she did most of the talking.

Things came to a head one evening during happy hour when they were two workers short and Hyacinth came in late again, unapologetic as usual.

"You're late again, Hyacinth," Selena said, annoyed, and was ignored.

She touched Hyacinth's arm as the woman started to breeze past her without answering. Next thing she knew she'd been slapped, shoved up against the side of the bar, and had a finger shoved so far up in her face that a few more inches and Hyacinth would've been digging into her nose.

"Look, woman, you jus' le me 'lone, see," Hyacinth cursed. "Ar-you mussa feel ah ar-you run this country. Well, non a ar-you nar come ya come tell me wha fu do. An' you cyan talk to whoever you want, but none ah ar-you cyarn put me outa bread, neither. If a pull-string run tings, me ha rope. An' ah ya fu me navel string bury, so me ha fu work."

Nobody jumped to Selena's defence, though everyone in the vicinity stood still and watched to see how things would play out.

Selena, never a fighter, was too shaken by the sudden attack to do more than stare as the side of the bar dug into her back and Hyacinth breathed into her face.

After a long minute, Hyacinth let her go and then went about her business as though nothing had happened. The other workers stared at her but none rushed over. One of the bartenders said, "You okay, Selena?"

She nodded.

The patron closest to them said, "You can't take that just so. Talk to Joey."

She did, and he promised to write Hyacinth a letter.

"A letter?" she asked, staring at him where he sat behind stacks of paper and files at his desk.

He looked kind of sheepish. "Look, I know Hyacinth troublesome, but just try and stay out of her way."

She didn't answer, couldn't speak.

"She's one of the best waitresses I have," Joey continued. "She been with me a long time."

"And if I tell you I refuse to work here with her still here?" she asked quietly.

"I'd tell you I don't respond well to ultimatums or threats," he said.

Then he sighed. "Look, Selena," he said. "I like you. The customers like you. I'd hate to see you go, but I can't just fire Hyacinth so. I'll tell her to stay out of your way. Any further problem with her, don't say nothing to her; just come to me directly and I will deal with it. Look, you shaken up, why you don't take the rest of the night off? Put some ice on your cheek. You'll still get paid for the night."

She left without further word. It was still light out so she walked the twenty-five minutes home, feeling trapped. She'd wanted to tell him and Hyacinth and all of them who'd just stood there what she thought of them, but the reality was she had rent due, two dependents, and she couldn't afford to stand on a soap box. It wasn't like there was Celia's salary to back her up any more.

Michael was at the house when she got there, as it seemed he was every night.

He was sitting in the front room with Silvano, the radio playing while Pamela sat on the floor nearby doing her homework.

Somehow, the whole scene made her even more sad, and she really couldn't say why.

She mumbled greetings then disappeared into her room, where Michael appeared only minutes later asking what was wrong. And she found she couldn't get the words out. She just felt so angry, and so trapped. She wanted to kick something, lash out at something, and he was there.

"I hate this stupid country," she said. "That's what's wrong. I hate stupid Antigua and stupid Antiguans with their pack mentality and blind prejudice. I hate it. I hate it here."

And, of course, he stood there, stunned and hurt. It had been a long time since she'd expressed any resentment or trepidation about her adopted home. His home.

She started crying finally, and he put his arms around her, in spite of the hurt she knew he must be feeling at her words and the fact that she was pushing against him.

"Calm down, calm down," he kept saying.

She cried a long time, until it felt like she was crying for everything that had ever gone wrong in her life.

"What's wrong? What happened?" he asked again, finally, when she had quieted down.

She shrugged, still in his embrace. "Rough night," she said, her voice hoarse.

"Want to talk about it?" he asked.

"Not really," she said. "Not right now."

33

Michael.

When she did get around to telling him what happened, he wanted to pound on somebody. First this Hyacinth person, then Joey for doing nothing. He figured the woman was either involved with Joey, or had been, or she was the consort or family of somebody "important".

Whatever the excuse, it was not enough in his eyes to excuse them treating his woman like that. He wanted to go out and do something to let them know she had somebody who cared about her, somebody they would have to deal with if they ever passed their place again.

She insisted against it, becoming increasingly agitated. "Michael, I still have to work there," she stressed.

"No you don't," he said. "We'll get you another job."

"Come on, Michael, there aren't a lot of them going around these days. If it wasn't for Asha, I wouldn't have gotten this one."

"I don't care," he said. "This is still not acceptable. If she do it once, she going to think she can do it again. I can't have that."

"You can't have that?" Selena retorted. "You're not the one with a child about to start pre-school and a sister to take care of, and rent to meet."

"So what? I don't know what it is to have responsibility?" he asked.

"Not like I do, no," she responded. "You still live in your mother house. That's one hell of a security blanket, no matter what your bills. I practically got pushed out of my mother's house, me and my sisters, so she could be rid of us."

He just stared at her like she was crazy. Finally, he sighed. "Look, Selena, I know you upset now, so I goin' let all that slide," he said. "But I not letting somebody assaulting you at your job, and your boss doing nothing about it, slide. I not letting that slide."

"You better. You have to. It's not your fight."

They fought on, well into the night. Pamela, surprisingly, did not interrupt, though they got very loud. And when it seemed she was tired of fighting, Selena threatened, pleaded, begged with him not to get involved. And, finally, the tears were there again, and he gave in. Or told her he did.

He got Hyacinth's last name from Asha, who got it from the bartender , with whom she'd been hanging out ever since she did the new mural at Joey's. He looked up her number and called her.

"I just want to tell you one thing: you ever lay hand on Selena Cruz again, is not she you goin' have to deal with, is me," he promised. "Everybody else might be afraid of you and your bully-bully ways, but not me. When I was fourteen, I lick a boy one lick with a two by four 'cross his shoulder for talking 'bout my mother. Selena is the woman I love, so don't think I wouldn't do at least as much to somebody who hurt her."

And he hung up on her in the middle of her spluttering and cursing.

Selena found out, of course. He knew she would, and he knew he'd broken a promise, but he knew he would've done the same thing again. He couldn't and wouldn't apologize for it. He didn't ever want to see her like she'd been that night.

He stared back at her, his lack of remorse clear in his eyes. She opened her mouth several times to speak, tried to look stern, but then just shook her head in a way a mother might have done with a child she just didn't know what to do with. And he smiled at her angry, retreating back.

34

Selena.

She stopped telling Michael about how things were going at her
job for fear that he would do something, if sufficiently disturbed,
to get her fired. Not that things were too terrible at work any more.
Hyacinth steered clear of her, and she steered clear of Hyacinth.

She started looking for other work in a vague, unfocussed sort of
way. Kind of the way her life felt lately.

Things came sharply into focus one night. The Roland Prince
Quartet was riffing on Thelonius Monk, and she was enjoying it,
the wind brushing her face as she stood outside under the stars on
a break. It wasn't a busy night. It never was when they played,
since people gravitated towards more contemporary tunes. But
she liked them; thought their music suited Joey's better, actually.
Anyway, Joey booked them a night a week – mid-week, which was
slow night. And she was enjoying them when she felt somebody
come to stand beside her.

"Selena, right?" a woman's voice said.

She did not want to open her eyes. She'd always believed she
was somewhat psychic, could tell when things were going to
happen. And right at that moment her eyes were struggling
against opening and facing this new unknown, even as her skin
grew cold.

"That's me," she said. "Can I help you?"

"No, just wanted to meet Michael's latest … woman."

And finally she did open her eyes to meet those of a beautiful,
dark-skinned woman. "You are?" she asked.

"Bethann," the woman replied. "Michael and I go way back."

"How do you know me? Michael never mentioned you to me,"
Selena said.

The woman shrugged. "Antigua's a small place," she said. "Plus,
I have a vested interest in knowing what Michael up to."

That last had her worrying. She really couldn't deal just then
with any notion of this Bethann person being pregnant by

Michael or any such soap-opera drama. She really couldn't. What she had with him was the one thing in her life that felt right just now.

"Are you getting to something?" she asked, too stressed by her worry for any more false politeness. "Because if you are I wish you'd hurry up and get to it."

"Eh-eh. Calm down. Just trying to be friendly," Bethann said, a little smirk twisting her lips. "Although I suppose I can understand your attitude. Lord knows I had to give enough women the cold freeze when I was Michael's … woman. But at the time he was either our next great West Indies hopeful or had just made the team, so they were coming out of the woodwork. I had to keep a watchful eye.

"I don't suppose you'd have the same kind of trouble these days. Although with him being on radio, who knows? Some people just looking for a celebrity screw, right? And all it takes to be a celebrity in Antigua is your voice on the radio, right?"

"What do you want?" Selena asked again.

"Just wanted to meet you," Bethann said. "I knew he was fishing around somebody, but I got real curious when he disappeared just after Deeno's Christmas Day party without another word. Wondered where he went, what he was up to. Went home to meet the family?"

She looked long at Bethann then said, "I have to get back to work now."

Bethann smiled, "Of course. It was nice meeting you."

Selena walked away, her thoughts in turmoil. She knew what the woman had been trying to tell her, but didn't want to face this other bit of her reality crumbling. So she smiled and went about her work. And when, after he left the radio station, Michael came to take her home, she said nothing about meeting his friend.

At home, she initiated sex, something she rarely did. And the timbre of their lovemaking was different, at least on her part, it had a desperate quality to it. It was hot. And afterwards, as he dozed, she felt tears burning her eyes.

Asha was in the bar the following night. To Selena, Michael's cousin looked different, seemed to have lost some of her edge. The bartender, Ricky, she occasionally smiled with and who chatted her up between customers seemed to have much to do with that. Selena wasn't one to subscribe to the view that a man could fix all that was hurting in a woman – in fact, experience had proven otherwise too often in her case – but in Asha's case, it certainly seemed to take the edge off.

She went over to her. "I don't think I ever told you," she said; "I love your mural."

Asha smiled cockily "Yeah, it adds something to the place, doesn't it?"

And Selena laughed in spite of herself.

"Where's Michael tonight?" Asha asked. "I got the impression he practically live down here since you started."

"Not quite," Selena joked back; and, with a knowing look, "Well, no more than you, anyway."

Asha smiled, "Well ..."

"My my, I can't believe it," Selena teased. "I have managed to embarrass Asha."

"Well, I am human after all," Asha said with a smile.

"Aren't we all?" Selena agreed, a little note of melancholy in her voice.

"Hm. I feel a weight of meaning behind those words," Asha said. Selena shrugged.

"Look, Selena ..."

And Selena laughed.

"What?" Asha asked.

"Nothing. Lately, every time someone says 'Look, Selena ...', I get worried."

Asha smiled. "Well, no need to worry," she said. "I was only going to say I know you've been grappling with a lot of things lately between Michael's confrontation with his father and ... that business with your sister – and, no, Michael didn't tell me all the details, but I knew it was enough to send you running home. I only go running home when I feel broken, and really, really broken at that.

"Anyway, with all of that, and starting over, the job ... the confrontation with The Bitch ...

"I know I don't come off as the warmest person – I've been told I should never run for office, because I'm not approachable. But I'm here if you ever want to talk. Okay? I mean, I don't promise wisdom. But I do have two ears."

Selena looked long at her, then nodded.

"Who's Bethann?" she blurted.

Asha just stared at her for a minute.

"Just a piece of trash from Michael's past," Asha said finally.

"If she's from the past, why is she coming here, dropping words for me?" Selena asked. But, before Asha could answer, Selena was called off her break by Joey, who'd come down from his office to wonder why no one was greeting the customers.

As she worked the rest of the night, she felt Asha's eyes on her from time to time, until, finally, Michael's cousin was gone. Michael came to get her near the end of her shift; said he'd just been five minutes away at Uncle Wellie's place. They went home. Again, she jumped him. Again, she cried herself to sleep.

35

Michael.

He broke the news to his mother first.
"I planning to marry Selena soon," he said over Sunday breakfast, or, rather, while he ate breakfast and she puttered around the kitchen.

"She pregnant?" was her immediate reply.

"No," he said, irritated. "Why you have to assume the worst?"

"So what's the rush?" she said.

"I thought you liked Selena," he said. "Now, you practically accuse her of trapping me. She don't even know yet what I have in mind. I just preparing you for it. Because if she accept, it means I goin' be moving out."

"Well," his mother said.

"I'll still help out as much as I can, but I need to have my own life," he said.

"Michael, I ever tell you not to have your own life?" his mother snapped. "What stupidness you chatting?"

When he told Asha she just stared at him.

"What? You knew this was coming," he said.

"I thought ... . Well, aren't you planning to leave your job soon?" she asked.

He had finally decided to make the jump to radio and concentrate his coaching on the upcoming camp and volunteer community activity. He was actually going on board at the station as a permanent member of its sports team, covering much more than cricket. Far from being a lowly reporter though, and being paid that salary, he was being brought in as a sports analyst.

"So, I'll be making more than I making now. People get married in less certain circumstances. I'm ready. And I feel we're ready."

"Okay," she said, finally.

"What, no trying to argue me out of it?" he teased.

"Is that what you want?" she asked seriously.

"No," he said. "I love Selena. I want to marry her."

"And you can be faithful to her?" she challenged.

"What, a man not allowed any mistakes in your book?" he demanded, irritated. "Of course, I can be faithful to her."

"Okay," she said. "Well, congratulations. You're a big man; you don't need me to argue you out of anything."

Uncle Wellie smiled. "Well, if you have to go, there are worse women you could go with," he teased.

Selena accepted. He'd expected to have to do a bit of convincing given her aversion to commitment. But she put up no roadblocks.

They made love that night, in a more gentle way than they had in a long time. It was satisfying, and he felt truly happy, like, finally, everything in his life was coming together.

36

Selena.

Life was hectic for Michael these days. It was one thing to host a show, another to be on board as a full-time analyst/commentator and correspondent and producer. He had to improve his knowledge of other sports, of reporting. He had to attend a lot of games. This amounted to Selena seeing much less of him than she was used to.

She had seen Bethann several times since the first, but managed to avoid her. Selena comforted herself with the notion that whatever the woman had been trying to insinuate, she was the one who would be shopping for a ring shortly with Michael.

She heard about a job teaching Spanish to Antiguans. It was only part time, however. Still, she was inclined to take it since they were less concerned with her educational certification than with her competency in both languages.

"I think you should take it," Pamela said.

"It's not going to pay all my bills," Selena insisted.

"So what? Look, if it will make you feel better, I can get something part time after school," Pamela suggested.

"No, your job is school," Selena said. "Besides, how much do you think you could make, and doing what, anyway?"

"Are you the same woman who, when Michael first came around, told him I couldn't play cricket because of all the money we were making crocheting doilies?" Pamela teased, prompting her sister to tug at a strand of her hair. They both laughed as they hadn't in a good while.

What made up her mind was another incident on the job. A man she later found out was a relation of the Prime Minister came on to her at work. He went from talking to putting his hands on her; she went from smiling to backing off and biting her tongue so hard it bled.

The bartender with whom Asha was going out filled her in on just whom she had rebuffed. "He have plenty money," he informed her.

She just looked at him, wondering again what Asha saw in him. Oh, there was no denying his effect on Asha, but sometimes Selena just found him to be so shallow.

She walked out of Joey's that night knowing she wouldn't be going back. She didn't like how she felt about herself working there, couldn't fake it any more.

"Maybe I can talk to Cecil again," she told Michael late that night when he came by after work. It was a clear night, the moon full-faced and bright. Silvano and Pamela had gone in for the night. They were sitting out on the porch. "I liked working there. I was by myself, I was learning about picture taking. He trusted me to run the office. He didn't care where I was from, that I wasn't from here."

Michael shrugged. "Maybe. He's not hot-headed. But once he get annoyed he don't turn it off easy, though."

"Yeah, I messed it up, I know," she acknowledged. "But if I had that job back, I'd feel a little better about things. With that job and the one teaching Spanish, I'd be more than able to meet my bills and the hours would still be better than Joey's. I've been worried about Pamela and Silvano alone here at night. Thieves. Boys coming around. She's at that age, you know. And she's so developed, she can seem older than she is."

"Pamela okay, man," Michael insisted.

"Easy for you to say. She's not your sister," Selena snapped. "I just don't want her having the same limited choice I, or even Celia, had."

He pulled her close against him. "We could start looking for a place together."

"What does that have to do with what we're talking about?" she asked, slightly irritated.

"Well, we still talking about our lives like one wouldn't have nothing to do with the other. My job, your job, your bills, your sister, my problems. Is not so no more. We need to start making some decisions anyhow."

"Michael, I can't think about this now," she said. "I have to decide …"

"We. We have to decide," he said. "You know, you're the one who said yes. Now, you acting like I forcing you to do something. You acting like this don't mean half as much to you as it does to me."

That's when she lost it a little bit, feeling hedged in. "You know what, Michael? Don't talk to me about what means more to whom," she lashed out. "You don't have the right to talk."

"I don't, I don't have the right ... what that supposed to mean? I don't ... wait ... Asha say something to you?"

She stared at him for a long time, feeling her heart breaking again. Finally, she said, "No, Asha's still your cousin. She didn't tell me anything about you and Bethann. You, on the other hand, just told me plenty."

He seemed at a loss for words, and she sighed heavily.

"Look, Michael," she eventually said. "Just leave me alone for a while."

He didn't even attempt to stop her; seemed frozen in fact, as she went inside and closed the door firmly behind her.

37

Michael.

He felt like somebody had punched him hard in the stomach. He felt numb and cold at first. Then he started warming up to his own indignation and anger. Fuck her and her games! Fuck Asha with her disloyal self! Then, after that, he just felt tired and sad, like something important was slipping away from him, and he couldn't figure out how to grab hold of it.

Finally, he felt shame at his own actions. He had messed this up. Only, admitting that didn't put him any closer to getting it back.

38

Selena.

Asha helped her get a second job at one of the Internet gambling companies. She worked an 11 p.m. to 6 a.m. shift. Which meant she was just getting in as Pamela left for school. But it also meant that, even with sleep, she got to spend most of the day with her son and some time with her sister before leaving for her evening teaching job.

Her non-Antiguanness was a non-factor in both cases. The gambling job meant she spent a lot of time on the phone. Asha moonlighted there as well, but her schedule changed a lot more than that of Selena, who preferred something steadier and didn't mind working the shift everyone dreaded.

She and Asha weren't exactly buddies, but Michael's cousin was just as annoyed with him over his screw-up and knew from her boyfriend why Selena had left her previous job. Whenever they were coming off shift together she'd give her a ride.

Michael came by a time or two trying to offer her a ride home, but she found she wasn't ready to deal with him. And the more time passed, the less, well, urgent it seemed.

It wasn't like she didn't miss him. She did. But she found herself wondering if it had really been love. Not that she would know love by looking at it. She'd been fooled before. But she couldn't understand why she felt so numb about the whole affair. Maybe because she'd had time to deal with her anger. She felt more disappointed than anything. She expected better of him.

So, okay, he couldn't talk to her or anyone at the time about what he was feeling. If all he wanted was to feel, why did he have to go somewhere else looking for sex? It wasn't like she held back on him. Maybe she didn't hold back enough. Well, at least, she consoled herself, she didn't have another baby out of the equation.

Bottom line, right now: she couldn't seem to work up the energy to deal with his remorse or his anger. He vacillated between the two, it seemed. Alternately trying to bully her and beg back. Men!

She missed him, though, had gotten used to his presence in her bed at night, even on the nights they didn't make love; especially on those nights. Talking back and forth in the dark, him holding her. It was a nice feeling having someone to come home to, to feel connected to someone where there was nothing demanded or expected. She missed that most.

Pamela missed him, too; that was plain. Her little sister was growing more and more silent, and she didn't like it; though, truth be told, it hadn't begun with this new hiccup in their lives. It went all the way back to Celia, and the demise of the cricket programme hadn't helped. The spirit Selena had once admired, once thought unflappable, had wavered some. She wondered if another trip home wasn't the fix they both needed.

Celia was there now. She'd learned this in the last letter from her mother. No mention had been made of Victor, except to say that Celia was alone.

She thought often of writing to, maybe even calling or emailing her sister. She had Internet access now, thanks to her job. She missed her younger sister. Knew she must have been hurt somehow by Victor, and, likely, couldn't talk to their mother or even their *tia* about it.

Besides, they were sisters, right? Men should never be allowed to come between that. Right?

Still, she procrastinated.

"How do you feel about a trip home when break comes up?" she put to Pamela.

But her baby sister only shrugged.

And there the subject rested.

The new twist in her life was Rico. Very good-looking in a compact, muscular Jon Seda way. Not tall like Michael but with very gentle features. She liked gentle in a man. He drove a taxi from the mall where the gambling company was based, and had offered her a ride a few times when she'd been stranded.

It was easy to be with him. They talked about home, falling into the easy familiarity of their own language. He even talked her into going to a show one weekend when she was off and a band from home was visiting.

He'd been in Antigua a lot longer than she had. Eleven years. Even had friends in high places, as he told her. The politician in his area saw him as something of a link to the huge Spanish community in his constituency.

She didn't much care for political intrigue so didn't pay much attention to all of that, however.

"So, Michael out of the picture?" her sister asked one evening as she got ready to go to work. There was a slightly accusatory tone in her voice.

"Michael and I need some time," was all she said.

"Meanwhile, you make time with somebody else," Pamela said. There was no mistaking that note of displeasure now.

"What, I can't have a friend?"

Pamela just gave her a look. And she felt then like she was the one who'd cheated instead of Michael. Her anger, thought long dead, revived at that.

She trailed after her little sister. "You know, I'm not the one who couldn't keep it tucked in," she argued.

"So what, nobody can make a mistake with you? One strike you're out, is that it?"

"That's not fair," she shouted back.

"It's true, though," Pamela argued. "First Celia, then Michael. Hey, maybe even Victor."

She felt like she'd been slapped. "What do you know anyway?" she said finally, turning away, heading back to her room.

It was Pamela's turn to follow her. "Right. I'm just a kid, right; what do I know? It's not like I have any real problems, right? But you know what, Selena? Everybody you push in and out of your life is pushed in and out of my life, too. And I'm tired of it. You can't choose for me that Celia's no longer my sister or Michael no longer my friend ..."

"I never tried to," she said whirling around.

"But that's what you did, isn't it?" Pamela challenged. "You didn't say it, you just did it. Just assumed that I would have your side in things."

"Not assumed; hoped," she said finally, sadly, "hoped that my sister would understand how much I had been hurt ..."

"You're not the first person to be hurt, Selena," Pamela said. "Get over yourself."

And she walked away, going to her room and pulling the door firmly closed behind her.

39

Michael.

He was surprised to see her there on his front porch when he got home, sitting with his mother. After over a month of her avoiding him, it was a bit of a shock.

"Can we talk?" she asked.

Despite it being what he'd been begging for, he wasn't quite sure he felt up to it just then. He'd spent most of the day at the hospital with Uncle Wellie, who'd taken seriously ill only that week, severely shaking up Michael's world. And he had to be at work in another hour or so. He'd hoped to just shut his eyes for five minutes.

"Sure," he said.

"Can we walk?" she asked, already heading out the gate past him. He followed, and they strolled like any couple out for an evening walk. It made him a little sad thinking how many times they'd done that when things had been so much better between them.

Despite her request, they walked a good stretch in silence.

In the quiet, he allowed himself that little leftover feeling of resentment at how Selena had shaken up his world as much with her absence as she had with her presence. He'd cursed out Bethann, before having her curse him out and tell him to grow up and stop blaming her for his own decisions; for her playing by the rules by which they'd always played. She was out of his life, for good, not just until the next time it was mutually convenient.

Things were strained between him and Asha. They'd spoken since, of course. They were family, after all, and she the only Lindo who had truly ever felt like family to him. But she was unapologetic about whatever part she'd played in Selena finding out about him. And though he'd acknowledged to himself that he had, in fact, screwed this up all on his own, he couldn't help feeling like a confidence had been broken.

Their most recent Sunday get-together had been a political roundtable that left him soured on his other friends, as well. Well, not so much Deeno, who was harmless and didn't have strong views about much of anything, but Meetoo, who in her efforts to reassure him that the break-up was all for the best, had gone on and on about how "them foreigners, especially them Santo Domingans, cost the opposition the last election anyway. And the thing is, when things get hot they can always go home," she said. "Meanwhile, we're stuck here."

Michael hadn't had the stomach for it, especially since it hardly applied to Selena, who wasn't political at all, and since it did nothing to fill the gaping space left in his heart and his life.

Later that night, he and Asha had talked, standing out on her balcony, before he left for home after barely touching dinner.

"You just have to give her time," she said.

"And what if that not enough?" he said, dejected enough in spite of his lingering resentment to seek the familiar comfort of his cousin and best friend's advice. "What if it just give her more time to stew over why I'm wrong for her?"

She shrugged at that. "Look, Michael, I don't have no track record to speak of, so I'm the last person to really be giving love advice," Asha said, "but I've been hurt by men, too. The healing either happen or it don't happen in its own time. You can't force it."

It wasn't what he'd wanted to hear; he was a man, hardwired to fix what was wrong. This wait-and-see, time-will-tell approach wasn't for him. But in the end, that was the only choice he'd been left with. Selena had very carefully stepped out of his life, and as much as he would've liked it to be otherwise, the rest, the coming back, the trusting again, was also up to her.

The lady in question seemed inclined to let the silence go on indefinitely, and he was just about to point out that he was going to be late for work in a little while when she spoke, finally.

"Look, I don't want anybody playing me for a fool," she said.

He sighed, not wanting to argue.

"Don't say you're sorry. I know you're sorry. I heard you the first five million times. Just … I don't want to be nobody's fool, doormat or hand cloth. I've been all those things and it wasn't fun the first time."

He sighed, not knowing what to say, not knowing how to make this right. But he needed her, had never needed anyone as much, especially now that the only father figure he'd ever been able to count on had been cut down, so to speak, by illness. He believed in her strength now, when at first all he had seen were her beauty and her gentle spirit. She was still beautiful, but there was wariness behind that beauty, and he regretted that he'd been the cause of any of it.

"I love you," he said. "I know I messed up, and I need to find a way, maybe for the rest of my life, to prove that to you, but I love you. More than that I need you."

She still hesitated. Finally, she said, "The thing is, walking away isn't as easy as I'd hoped. Not even in the interest of self-preservation. You've become a part of me. More than that, you've become a part of the most important thing to me, my family. Even so, even so, I not prepared to ..."

"I don't want you to," he rushed to assure her. She looked at him a long, long time. Then gave a little nod.

They walked some more, trying to settle things between them. But they knew it couldn't all be done in one conversation.

He told her about Uncle Wellie, and she was with him the next time he went to visit, holding his hand as they walked down Hospital Hill, silently acknowledging what they'd both seen – the sidling up of death.

"He made me who I am," he confessed to her as they sat in the shadow of a large and ancient tree at the Botanical Gardens. "You know, with my father absent, and my mother lost in her pain and regret, he was the only person who made me feel happy and, you know, interested in things. Pulled me out of my shell."

He laughed then on a realization, "I been moaning all this time 'bout the father I didn't have. Truth is, I had one of the best fathers anybody could want. Fuck that weak bastard! I don't know why I let him get to me like that. Uncle Wellie was more than enough."

He really believed it this time, said it with conviction.

In the next minute, he grew despondent on another thought. "I can't imagine him not being, you know. Just 'poof,' no more. I can't even wrap my mind around that."

And then she held him as he cried, and he held on to her like she was his anchor, never wanting to let her go.

Uncle Wellie didn't last long; as suddenly as the illness had come on, it claimed him.

Selena and Pamela were with Michael at the burial, as was his mother, and Asha, and not much of anyone else. But he found he didn't need much else.

He went back to Selena's place that night and they made love for the first time since their rift; easy and gentle, and so good. He never tired of her; her responsiveness, compared to her usually reserved demeanor, like an aphrodisiac. Tonight, it was a little more for him. He felt connected to her again, and he felt alive.

He left her bed that night only because she made him, wanting him to check on his mother.

"Why?" he'd asked.

"She lost her brother; she might need someone," Selena said.

That surprised him a little bit. Yes, Uncle Wellie was his mother's brother, but he'd always thought of him as his. Uncle Wellie and his mother rarely saw each other, though his uncle did inquire about her every time they got together.

In that moment of shock, he had to admit that he'd never seen his mother as a real person with nuances and complexities. He had to admit that he'd never really attempted to breach the barriers she put up, to know her. He wondered if she saw him the same way.

He found her sitting alone in the kitchen, only the light two rooms away in the living room reducing the gloom somewhat.

"Mammy, you okay?" he asked.

She didn't answer right away. "Mammy?"

"So, where you been, by her?" his mother asked, radiating something that seemed like anger.

"Yes," he said.

"So, she's all the family you have now?"

"No," he said, annoyance stirring a little at that.

His mother got up then and went to her room, closing the door firmly, leaving him wondering what the hell had just happened.

The following day, he began going through Uncle Wellie's stuff. When the landlord came around to ask him about how long it'd take him to get the things out, he impulsively responded that he was keeping the place. Hell, he'd been meaning to get his own place anyway, and he'd always felt more at home here than anywhere. Besides, he'd need time to go through all of Uncle Wellie's belongings without some landlord breathing down his neck. Added to that, he didn't know what to make of his mother, and figured that more than anything they needed space.

40

Selena.

The night of the funeral, after they'd made love and she'd sent him home, she wrote a letter. To Celia.

There was a part of her that kicked Michael out that night because she needed a little space. He was eager to go back to the way things were, and leaning on her during his Uncle Wellie's deterioration and death had accommodated that presence. But bits and pieces of her still hurt, still felt anger; and she needed to take her time healing from the sting of his betrayal.

But with him there again, she had to admit to herself that she craved him as much as he craved her, missed him, loved him. And, Lord knows, Pamela was happy to have him back in their lives, and seemed to be holding it together a little better.

That had been her incentive to go to him or, at the very least, to examine what remained of her feelings for him. She'd discovered that beneath the numbness there was quite a hurricane of emotional activity needing to be confronted. She had been forced to give herself a good hard look in the face of her sister's anger, upon seeing her usually resilient sister crumble in the face of the pile-up of losses and changes. And part of her wanted this to work for that reason even now. But the truth was, though she knew she could carry on if things didn't work out between them, she wanted them to, because she did still love him.

Still, she found she needed to control the pace of things, and that had been part of her reason for pushing him out that night. And she did think his mother just might need him. She knew Michael didn't think of his mother as a real person; she was his mother, defined by what she expressed and not by the many other things she couldn't. And, maybe she was projecting, but Selena felt her realness, her humanness, and knew that she might need her son that night.

Just as, she found, she was needing her sister. Celia, not Pamela. Ever since her fight with Pamela, she'd been thinking about Celia even more than usual.

That night, she wrote her a letter. It began traditionally enough, inquiring after her health and well-being, before disintegrating into a diatribe of hurt and anger. It was cathartic. She tore that letter up, and tried another, one a little bit more restrained. She fished out an envelope and promised herself to mail that one, to reopen the lines of communication to the best friend of her childhood and one to whom her ties could never be severed.

She helped Michael move into Uncle Wellie's, gave him some crocheted doilies, helped him shop for curtains. He kept suggesting that they try living together, but she wasn't ready for that yet.

41

Michael.

He liked being around Uncle Wellie's sculptures. "The Bugler", a slave rebellion piece. "The Long Walk", which showed a silhouette of a woman – seemingly naked and with long flowing hair and a bucket piled on her head, sashaying her way home – "presumably from a standpipe at a nudist colony," Michael thought with a smirk. "Riddim" featured a pan player merging with his instrument and his music.

He was seriously considering putting on a show of his uncle's work and had even spoken informally with Ms. Mills at the museum about it. She was open to the idea, as she said she was keen on showcasing local culture and history.

He'd always felt that Uncle Wellie had short-changed himself by not exposing his art. He wondered what the old man would say about his plans. No, actually he knew his uncle would accuse him of dipping into people's affairs, and ask please to be left to rest in peace.

Sitting in the ruins of Fort James looking out at the sea, one of their favourite thinking and talking spots, Michael smiled to himself at this. Stop being so afraid is what he would have told his uncle, in turn; believe in your talent.

It was his uncle pushing him that had got him onto the Windies team in the first place. It baffled him that the man would do any less for himself, when, as far as he was concerned, his uncle's talent surpassed the nephew's little skill.

Michael discussed his plans, with, of all people, his mother.

She seemed somewhat non-committal at first, but soon had taken over the idea. She was down at the museum constantly pushing for a date, then pushing for the necessary support and promotions. She oversaw the transportation of the pieces, the display of the work, and so on. Michael was baffled.

"I don't know why you're so surprised," Selena said. "He was her brother."

But Michael had never seen his mother throw herself into anything with such zeal. Of course, she wasn't keen on dealing with the media, and he had to handle that part of it. There was some interest, given his local not-quite-celebrity status first on the field and now on the airwaves, so the showing went well. People wanted to buy, but he found he wasn't committed to the idea of selling. Every piece was so much a part of his uncle. He thought he understood Uncle Wellie better at that point; that maybe it wasn't fear or lack of confidence in his talent that kept him from pushing forward but his unwillingness to part with what were essentially pieces of his soul.

In the end, Michael kept most of the pieces, selling a few to those he deemed to be true art lovers and collectors. It was hardly a scientific approach. He knew he needed to make space at his new home. But it was still too fresh. Maybe in time, he told himself.

42

Selena.

Celia responded to her letter, expressed her desire to come back to Antigua. Victor was gone from her life, she said. She was pregnant, things were just too difficult at home, and she was uncomfortable in her mother's house. She practically begged to come "home". Selena felt torn. Part of her yearned to mend fences with her sister, part of her just couldn't let it go.

It was a hurt so deep she couldn't speak even to Michael or Pamela about it. Pamela, meanwhile, had started dating. The boy was Spanish with Antiguan roots; his family was among those who'd migrated to the Dominican Republic many years ago, and were only now finding their way back home. He'd even reconnected with distant relatives in Antigua. He was a little older than her sister, and nice enough. So Selena tried to be a big sister and not a mother hen, and an oppressive one at that.

But it wasn't easy. Part of her just wanted to wrap her baby sister up, and lock her away from all the heartache she knew would surely come before her life was over. Once you got tangled up with men – even the ones who said they loved you, or the ones who truly meant it even when they couldn't say it – pain was inevitable.

When she went to Michael's that evening Deeno was there, drinking beer and hanging out on the front porch. She'd never liked him, had told Michael so, in fact. But now, his presence just reminded her of Bethann and what took place that night between her and Michael either during or after his little party. It was unfair, perhaps, but it was how she felt.

Her coldness soon had him on his way, and she had Michael to herself, sitting on the porch, sipping beer and wondering what to do about Celia. She got a little buzzed by the beer that night, and found it was just what she needed to put things down for a while. That night their lovemaking was like a full dance – a slow dance quickening to mid-tempo rhythms, segueing into something quicker, like Burning Flames' "Keep it so", and finally the gentle recline of after-play. She liked that about Michael, that he didn't roll over and go to sleep immediately after sex. He didn't talk much, but she didn't need that; just his hand caressing a bare arm, or massaging her scalp; just him.

"I love you," she told him, before she knew herself that she was going to say it. And he went still, then let out a breath, echoing her words on his next breath. He pulled her tighter, and she knew then that he'd been as worried as she that they wouldn't make it despite best intentions, that the cut was too deep to simply scab over and heal.

But she knew this: despite the lingering hurt, she felt complete when they were together. And when they made love, her world didn't rock like the romance novels promised; it stilled, providing calm even in the stormiest of times.

"I love you," she repeated, softer this time, but he had already drifted to sleep.

43

Michael.

Selena, Silvano and Pamela went home in late summer, mere weeks before Pamela, who had participated in Michael's community cricket camp and then had insisted she wanted to stay in Antigua for Carnival, had to be back at school.

He had to work, and couldn't manage the time. He was a little worried since Selena had assured him she would speak to Celia while she was there, lay things to rest between them. The possibility existed that her sister might return to Antigua with her, and he wasn't sure how he felt about that.

Actually, that he knew exactly how he felt was the problem. He had no doubt that if Celia had been around when Selena discovered his screw-up, a reconciliation would've been out of the question. She'd have hammered into Selena's consciousness that he was just living up, or down, to his potential, fuelling Selena's own doubts. He thanked God for small favours. Those few months without Selena, and even the uncertainty after they'd got back together, had been hellish enough.

He went to his mother for Sunday breakfast now. The tension between them, the cause of which still baffled him, had eased somewhat since the exhibition of Uncle Wellie's sculptures. He'd found the experience personally fulfilling and, though they'd never discussed it, suspected she had too.

"I'm thinking of asking Selena to marry me," he told her on Easter Sunday over saltfish, antroba and salted cucumber after they'd both returned from church. It was just the two of them, the godchild having long since left, of her own volition, to go back to her mother.

She was sitting at the table with him for a change, and said, "I thought you did that already."

He shrugged at that, not wanting to go down that road.

"Well, I hope you don't screw it up this time," she said finally. "Lord knows it in your blood."

"Don't say that; I'm nothing like him," he retorted.

She raised a brow at that. "And what you know 'bout him?"

"I met him," he said. "He's weak. I'm not weak. I'm a man."

She looked stunned at this, and just stared at him for a long time. "Weak?" she mused, finally. "Well, he was little more than a boy. I was little more than a girl, myself. Probably would've run, too, if I could."

"I don't think so," Michael said.

She shrugged.

"Besides," Michael went on, "it was about more than him being a boy. It was about him being less than a man. A man faces up, even when he screws up. It was after Uncle Wellie died that I realized how much I'd learned from him about being a man. As long as I had him, I was never without a father. And you know what else? I may not always have appreciated it, but I owe you plenty too."

She didn't respond to this. He sensed that she just didn't know what to say to his ramblings.

"And I'm not talking about you shoving me in their faces, refusing to let them forget about me or brush me under the carpet. I'm talking about what you taught me about facing up," he said.

She laughed bitterly at this. "Don't put me down for sainthood yet."

He cut her off. "Yeah, yeah, you didn't have a choice about staying; he did. Maybe you'd have made the same choices he did given half a chance. I heard you. But that kind of speculation is pointless."

Tears came to her eyes then. "You know, I came to Antigua when I was a young girl," she said, whisper-soft like she was still in the confessional. "Wellie was much older than me, nineteen by then; and my mother, who had her own handful, sent me to live with him. Kind of like your girl, Selena, and her younger sister. I don't know why she picked me. I know I resented it; felt like it would be worth living in any kind of poverty than to be without my mother; than to be the one she thought she could do without.

"Looking back now, I realize that she just wanted better for me, and maybe even thought I was the one most suited to make use of my opportunities. In time, we all got scattered anyway; this one to Canada, that one to England, that one to bush country somewhere. Wellie was the last one I had who I even knew where he was or what he was up to. Mammy gave me that; didn't just send me off to strangers. Gave me to family.

"But I resented her, I resented Wellie, and in true teenage fashion I was a real handful. But much as I had a lot of man friend and hung out a lot, I never slept around. I was a virgin when I had sex with your father ..."

Typically, Michael felt himself blush at the mention of his mother having sex, but forced himself to keep still; not to break whatever spell had loosened her tongue.

"That was a rough-rough time. Wellie put me out. Didn't know that, eh? When I got pregnant with you, he put me out; said if I was woman enough to take man, I was woman enough to make it on my own ..."

Michael found himself wanting to protest this conflicting image of his uncle, but again he forced himself to remain still. With effort.

"... We reconciled, in a way, down the road, but we were never really close. I mean, we never had been, I guess; but he was family. And from the time you were old enough to be decent company, he took you under his wing. I thought that was a good thing; good for you to have a man in your life. So I allowed it though I still harboured some resentment.

"Besides, that was what people did then with girls who had shamed their families; punished them even more. I remember I had a time finding a place to stay; all my so-called friends showed their colours then. Your father's mother was the worst. Why her son, she wanted to know. Her son was from a good family, destined for great things; why I must choose him to tie down? As much as I throw roun' myself, any and all breed of mortal could've been the father, she said.

"God had the last laugh, though, when he take his face self and put on you. Even she could see that for herself, and then shame alone force her to accept you a kind of how. And I never asked her or him for a cent; not that they ever offered. But I show them that I push through, get you a good education, live to see you achieve great things."

Michael wanted to interject then, still conflicted about his so-called achievements.

"Yes, I know you've stumbled," she went on as though anticipating his objection. "But the stumbling don't take 'way from the stepping. How many men get called up to play for West Indies, hm? But you did! And look what you doing now. All on your own merit; not because of the Lindos or nobody else, but because of you. Because of you!

"Much as she think of herself, little as she thought of me, I didn't raise no low-class, low-minded Antiguan looking for no handout. I raised somebody determined to make his own way. And as I learned the hard way, stumbling is a part of life."

His mother looked so much older and tired to him then. And he realized he'd never seen a picture of her as a girl. Had never seen that teenager, liming and hanging out and acting out. He felt sad about that, but better for having heard her out, even if the conversation had left his uncle with a somewhat tarnished halo.

She got up to clear up the dishes then, did that in silence, then made to leave the kitchen.

"Mom," he said, stopping her. "What you think about Selena? About me and her getting married?"

"Junior, that's your decision," she said.

"I know," he retorted, somewhat annoyed. "I know it's my decision. But what do you think of that decision? I mean, sometimes I think you're okay with her, and sometimes, like after the funeral, you seem to resent her."

"Resent her?" she said, annoyed. "I was alone and feeling sad the night of my brother's funeral, Michael."

Still, he felt that wasn't the entire truth, but he suspected he had got as much confession as he was likely to get out of his mother. It was more than he'd ever got, her programmed lamentations to no one in particular notwithstanding.

"So you think me marrying her is ... ?" he pushed, going back to his original question.

"I think is your life," she said, then after a pause gave a little. "I think she's a decent girl. She have a good heart, anyway. You could do worse."

The way her words echoed Uncle Wellie's made him smile. Such romantics, he thought, his mother and his uncle.

44

Selena.

She and Silvano stayed with her *tia* during the short visit home. Pamela stayed at their mother's, where Celia and her baby girl, Mariposa, were, as well.

The baby was a delight; not too much of her father's looks in her, for which Selena was happy. It would have made things that much harder.

She and Celia were painfully polite to each other, though watching her with the baby – Victor's baby – stirred some residual resentment. They didn't talk much, until one night when she went by and the lights were out, Silvano and Mariposa asleep, Pamela out, and her mother in bed early thanks to a flu bug. Children flitted around in the dark street, and she and Celia sat out, drinking beer and soda, and talking in the language of their home.

Celia confessed she didn't know where Victor was, that he hadn't treated her well, that maybe they hadn't been good for each other after all.

"No shit," Selena thought, but didn't say.

"I don't want to stay here," Celia said. "I don't want to end up like *Mami*. Until she was real and in my arms, God help me, I didn't even want my baby, my Mariposa. I thought about getting rid of her, but couldn't bring myself to do it before it got to be too late. Then she came, and she was the only beautiful thing left of something I was very ashamed of. I was most ashamed that I had chosen him over my sister."

Selena didn't respond to this.

"I want to come back to Antigua," Celia said, not for the first or the second or the third time. "I could leave Mariposa with *Mami* for a while, then send for her. I don't know. Sometimes, I think I couldn't stand to be away from her, other times I think it would be for the best. I don't even know if Antigua is really the right place any more, but I can't stay here, and I won't be going back to the Virgin Islands."

Selena looked hard at this unfamiliar uncertainty in a sister who'd always had, if nothing else, the conviction of her opinions. She thought to herself: this is what men – no, not men – men like Victor, did to you. They robbed you of your sense of self. Even during their most difficult times, being with Michael had never left her feeling as adrift from herself as her sister seemed now.

"You don't need my permission to come back, Celia; if you want to come back, come back," she said finally on a sigh.

"I want to make sure things are okay between us," Celia confessed.

Selena sighed fully then. "Celia, I think that might take more than one conversation and a few beers. You were there through all my shit with Victor. You harbouring him, going off with him, having his child, hurt more than I can ever express to you."

Her sister didn't answer that. "Look," Selena said finally. "In time, I hope things will be easier between us. But I can't give you absolution if that's what you're looking for. And, like I said, you don't need my permission to come back to Antigua."

"Need a place to stay," Celia said, quietly.

"Well, I'm not too certain about that. Everything else aside, I'm planning on moving in with Michael ..."

"So, he's still in the picture ..."

"Yes, he's still in the picture," Selena said, irritated. "He might not be a perfect man in many, many ways. But, you know what? I'm not a perfect woman, and this world is not perfect. I won't say that he hasn't hurt me in the past, won't maybe hurt me again; but for once the love hurt less than the hurt, you know, and it doesn't leave me feeling naked."

Celia didn't respond right away. When she did, it was to ask, "So he asked you to move in with him?"

"Well, yes, a long time ago, to move in with him, to marry him. I've been dragging my feet for various reasons. He hasn't asked recently. But I feel ready to do it now, so I think I might do the asking this time around," Selena explained.

"Oh," Celia said.

They sat in silence for another long stretch.

"Well, maybe Mariluz; maybe I could stay with her until I get a job, a place," Celia said. "Maybe I could give you a letter to take back. In that case, it would definitely be best to leave the baby here with *Mami* for a while."

"You've spoken to *Mami* about this?"

"No," Celia admitted, "but she won't refuse me this; I know that."

"Well, it's your decision," Selena said.

At that point, Pamela came walking up the street in the dark, a ghostly shadow in the darkness.

She started babbling about her visit with her friends, her boyfriend in Antigua, school; simply happy, Selena suspected, to see her sisters together and talking. Maybe, in time, she mused, it would all feel right again.

For the moment, though, she let her mind drift away to where she really wanted to be, at home with Michael. When had Michael become home, she wondered. But then, what did that matter? Even with all they'd been through and the hard adjustments to life in Antigua, the realities of loving this particular Antiguan man, she found that he just was that: home.

Glossary

antroba	eggplant
bull-bud	bull pistle, a long tough whip made of a bull's penis
dumps	small, yellowish-green fruit with single seed
dutty foot	loose woman
mussa	must
pull-string	influential connection
scrunchy	hair-tie
sweats	sweatsuit
turkleberry	or turtleberry: tree with sticky seed used as glue
ya	here